ANY GIVEN SUNDAY

MARI CARR

MONDAY'S CHILD

Monday's child is fair of face,
Tuesday's child is full of grace,
Wednesday's child is full of woe,
Thursday's child has far to go,
Friday's child is loving and giving,
Saturday's child works hard for a living,
But the child who is born on the Sabbath day,
Is bonny and blithe and good and gay.

~Traditional nursery rhyme

PROLOGUE

"Where's Chad?" Lauren asked breathlessly as they entered Sean's apartment.

Sean rested his forehead against hers for an extra second or two before pulling away from the kiss they'd just shared. However, the distance was too much for him and the image of her in her mini-skirt and silky blouse proved to be his undoing. He pressed her against the door to steal another long, hot kiss. They'd gone out for a romantic dinner to celebrate the end of their first month as a couple.

"Chad's out for the night," he replied. He grasped her hand and lifted it to his lips, placing a kiss on her palm. "Thanks for making sure I made it to the door safely, Ms. Chase," he teased. She'd followed him up to his apartment, jokingly claiming it was the gentlemanly thing to do after driving them home from the restaurant. "Do you need to leave right now or do you want to hang out for a while?"

He was unwilling to say goodbye to her after such a great evening.

She smiled and ran her hand down his chest. "I'm not in any hurry."

They'd been friends forever, so there was no awkwardness between them. Years as best friends had bred a comfortable familiarity. It had also built up some pretty deep-seated need in Sean. If he didn't get her into his bed soon, he was likely to do himself an injury. Sporting a hard-on 24/7 couldn't be good for anybody.

Sean stole another kiss and wondered if he'd ever experienced anything so amazing in his life. "Good. You wanna watch TV or make out?"

She laughed. "I wanna have sex."

Her quick response took Sean off-guard for a second, but he was accustomed to her forthright, honest nature. It was refreshing and, in some ways, a relief. He was part of a large family that walked to the beat of a different drummer. Sometimes he worried their quirkiness was hard for outsiders to take. It was cool to just be himself—Collins warts and all—and not have to worry about scaring her away because of his unconventionality.

"Jesus," he muttered and she gave him a husky laugh that was sexy as hell.

He studied her face and saw his own feelings reflected in her eyes—the look was hungry, almost feral. "I want you so much," he confessed, running the back of his hand along her soft cheek. She was the most gorgeous woman he'd ever seen. "I've wanted you forever."

She nodded. "The feeling's mutual."

She grabbed the hem of his T-shirt and pulled it over his head before he could respond. He wasn't surprised to discover this aggressive side. Lauren was a strong-willed, opinionated woman and it stood to reason she'd attempt to take the lead in the bedroom. Leaning forward, she planted several wet kisses on his chest before using her teeth to playfully bite his pec.

He pulled away, grasping her face between his hands, and spoke the words dying to escape. "I love you."

Her breath caught at his admission and he heard her gasp. It was the first time either of them had used the words. Maybe it was too soon to speak them, but he didn't care.

"I love you too."

He smiled, the happiness in his soul too big for his body. Though they hadn't revealed their transition from friends to couple yet, Sean was anxious to scream it to the world. He'd found the woman of his dreams. He turned around and bent down. "Climb on."

"A piggyback ride?" she asked, laughing. He'd been giving her piggyback rides for years. It had started one day when she got a splinter in her foot at the pier by the lake where she'd been swimming with him and Chad. Since then, whenever the mood struck them, she'd climb on and he'd race around with her holding on for dear life. She made him laugh, made his life fun.

"Dear God, only you would whisk a woman off to the bedroom with a piggyback ride."

"You prefer the fireman's hold?" He started to turn around again but she stopped him.

"Nope. This works."

Giggling, she climbed onto his back and he carried her to the bedroom. They'd been hesitant to spend too much time together in his apartment, usually holding their make-out sessions at her place. Sean wasn't sure what was keeping Lauren from broadcasting the changed nature of their relationship to everyone. As for him, it was only his roommate, Chad, from whom he felt the need to hide the truth.

He felt guilty, though he couldn't understand why. Lauren and Chad had never been more than friends, but sometimes when he looked at the two of them together, as they studied or simply watched television, Sean wondered if Chad would feel he had betrayed him somehow.

Sean backed up to his bed and dropped her onto the mattress. She laughed as she bounced, but the sound was short-lived when he turned around and crawled on top of her. They'd done some pretty heavy petting the past few weeks and covering her delicate frame never failed to provoke an intense response inside him. He was hornier than he'd ever been in his life. He kissed her hard.

"Hurry," she whispered.

Sean felt the slight urge to call her to task for trying to guide this experience. He was used to calling the shots in bed, but Lauren would struggle with handing over so much control. It didn't help that she knew him as affable and easygoing. An uncomfortable awareness crept in. There was very little he wouldn't do for her—even hiding his more dominant nature in the bedroom.

He pulled away from her and they undressed with haste, kissing and touching each newly revealed body part, each naked bit of skin.

By the time they lay down once more, he felt as if he had a fever. His body was flushed, aching, his cock full to bursting.

"God, please," she moaned when he put his mouth against her pussy. His tongue tormented her clit and he knew she needed to be filled.

"Sean," she said, her fingers grasping his hair tightly, painfully, as she tried to direct him, to move him to where she needed him most. "Inside me."

He looked up at her. Tried to convey with a look the words he couldn't say. This moment was too perfect.

"Please," she whispered, and he was surprised by the slight tremor in her voice.

Sean rose, coming over her body and kissing her gently. "I'll never hurt you, Lauren."

She returned his kiss. "I know."

He quickly donned a condom and when he pushed inside her, for the first time in his life he felt true love.

He made sure each thrust was deep and easy as she grew accustomed to his girth. He ran his fingers through her soft red hair, kissing her as they moved together. Her hands touched him everywhere—his shoulders, his arms, his face. Her delicate fingers stroking his skin drove his arousal even higher and he fought not to come too soon.

The moment was too perfect, too long overdue, and he wanted to make it last a lifetime or three.

When her first orgasm came quickly, it took them both by surprise.

He smiled and kissed her gently. "Looks like we're compatible everywhere. Wanna go for a two-fer?"

"God," she cried, when he continued to move in her body. "Yes."

He reached down and touched her clit, applying pressure, relishing the feeling of her movements below him. She was out of control, writhing on the bed and lifting her hips to meet his thrusts. The strength of her desire was contagious and, for a moment, he felt lightheaded as even more blood rushed to his cock.

He brought her to climax once more, his movements growing less calculated, more frantic as he came closer to finding his own release. When she wrapped her legs around his waist and met him blow for blow, he knew he was a goner.

He came and the power behind his climax felt strong enough to derail a train.

She sighed contentedly when he pulled free, gathering her closer.

As they lay in each other's arms, sleep coming to claim them, Sean turned to kiss her on the brow. "I want to tell people about us."

She nodded once. "It's time," she agreed.

For a brief moment he considered making the confession that was on the tip of his tongue, but the words wouldn't come. There was one secret he could never tell her. Never tell anyone. Silently, he prayed it wouldn't come back to destroy the bond they'd just forged.

"Tomorrow." He tightened his grip on her. "We'll tell everyone tomorrow."

Her breathing slowed, became softer when she drifted off to sleep.

A sound in the hallway distracted him from saying more. He listened to Chad's footsteps walking away from the room. His heart stuttered slightly as Chad's door closed with a soft click.

Sean's mind whirled over the evening, considering how it was possible to experience utter happiness and absolute sadness at the exact same time.

Lauren loved him. Sex with her rocked his world. He'd promise her forever and mean it.

All those things were true. However, there was one other truth—a bigger truth—tarnishing this moment.

Chad was on the wrong side of the door.

CHAPTER ONE

*T*wo *years later...*

"Okay, that box goes in the kitchen," Lauren said, directing Killian and her Pfaltzgraff dishes to the last available bit of space on the island counter. She grinned. She'd always wanted a kitchen with an island.

"Thanks again for helping us move, K." She smiled as Killian Collins gave her a wink.

"Beats the hell out of working. We're at the roofing phase on our latest job site and believe me, it was no hardship to leave that task to someone else."

"I really don't think we could have done this without you and the other guys."

"Hey, K. Where are you?" Killian's twin brother, Tristan, called from the hallway.

"They found me." Killian grimaced before yelling, "In the kitchen."

"Come give me a hand with this box. Fucker is heavier than shit."

Killian shrugged. "Duty calls."

Male voices calling directions to each other sounded from all around the house. Lauren followed Killian out of the kitchen to check their progress. She and Sean had loaded the pickup trucks of every friend and relative they had and started the big move at the crack of dawn. Now it was just after noon. She was starving and exhausted.

She took a calming breath as she watched the Collins men lugging furniture and boxes into her new home. She and Sean were moving into a house in a quiet suburb on the outskirts of Baltimore with their best friend, Chad. She should be excited, happy. And for the most part she was, but there was also a niggling little feeling that kept nagging at the back of her mind, telling her something wasn't quite right.

She'd dated Sean for two years. Moving in together was clearly the next step in their relationship. She'd been thrilled when he'd found this house and asked her to share it with him. Unfortunately, she couldn't shake the odd feeling something wasn't quite right. She wondered if she was rushing into this new stage before she was ready.

She grimaced as she looked around the new house filled boxes. Everything would be fine once they unpacked and got into a routine.

It's just cold feet.

"Foosball table coming through," Sean called out as he and Chad made their way down the hall.

Lauren blocked his path. "Where do you think you're heading with that?"

"Dining room."

She shook her head and pointed to the right, in the opposite direction of the dining room. "Office."

He and Chad put the table down despite the groan of protest from Tristan, who'd been following them with two large lamps in his hands.

Sean gave her an exasperated look. "Lauren, we already discussed this. There's a table in the kitchen and you know that's where we're eating. The dining room is gonna be wasted space. How in the hell are you going to get any work done in an office with a foosball table in it? Think of the temptation."

She smirked. "I don't find foosball to be a temptation."

Chad toyed with one of the plastic players on the table. "Well, I do, and I don't want my GPA slipping this late in the game. We're only a couple of semesters away from getting our doctorates."

"Sean, we're moving into this house because we decided it was time to grow up, to leave the college scene behind and start working toward a solid future. A foosball table in the dining room sort of defeats that purpose. Besides, it only has to stay in the office until you guys finish fixing up the basement. Chad wants it down there with him."

Sean moved closer to her and tugged her ponytail playfully. "Why don't we compromise? We'll put it in the dining room until we get a dining table. After that, we'll move it to the office."

She considered his compromise and decided it was a fair one. They'd already made plans to buy a table later in the week, so she wouldn't have to wait long. "You promise?"

Sean crossed his heart, laughing. "I'll even seal the deal with a kiss." He leaned forward and placed a soft kiss on her lips. Even after two years with Sean, her heart began to race the second his lips touched her.

"I promise too," Chad added as they started by her. He placed a quick kiss on her cheek and wiggled his eyebrows. Her libido kicked into overdrive despite her attempts to keep it in check. Not cool. She should *not* get hot and bothered every time Chad touched her. She was head over heels in love with Sean.

Still...

She stepped out of the way as they continued toward the dining room, Tris at their heels.

"Nice house."

Lauren turned around and spotted Sean's sister, Riley, and her husband Aaron coming in with more boxes. "When did you two get here?" Lauren asked.

"Just now. Thought we'd grab some stuff off the truck and start helping." Riley turned around and put her box on top of the heavy one Aaron was already carrying. "These say books, so I'm assuming they go in the office we just passed."

Lauren nodded, confirming Riley's assumption.

"Put those in there, sugar, while Lauren gives me the tour."

Aaron groaned. "If I fucking pull a muscle, Riley, you'll be sorry. Probably be laid up for weeks. No boom-boom."

Lauren laughed at Aaron's taunt as Riley started to grab her box back. Aaron chuckled and moved away before she could retrieve it.

"Gotcha," he teased as he walked to the office.

"Asswipe," Riley muttered, though her face betrayed the truth. Lauren didn't think the honeymoon would ever end for those two. They'd eloped in Vegas over two years earlier, but they still only had eyes—and hands—for each other.

"Thanks for coming over to help, Riley. I really do appreciate it. Actually, I don't know how we could have moved all this stuff if it weren't for your family."

Riley took her arm and propelled her up the stairs. "Gotta be some perks to having four overgrown, over-bearing brothers. Top of that list is that they can move all the heavy shit. So we'll start the tour upstairs. What are the sleeping arrangements?"

Lauren led her toward the first room at the top of the stairs. "Sean and I have the master bedroom and until the guys finish building the basement apartment for Chad, he'll be in the guest room."

"Mmm hmm," Riley hummed.

Lauren tried to figure out what was going on in the woman's head. She'd been making odd comments about this move ever since they'd announced it to Sean's family. Lauren suddenly wondered if she hadn't been as good at hiding her secret lust for Chad as she'd thought.

"This is the master bedroom. It has a great bathroom through those doors—big-ass Jacuzzi tub and everything." Then she sighed at the pile of boxes lining the walls, the dismantled king-sized bed and the drawer-less dressers. God only knew where the drawers had ended up. "Jeez. It's gonna take ages to get this place put together."

Riley was standing at the doorway, looking down the hall. "Where is Chad sleeping again?"

"A little farther down the hallway, on the right. The guest bathroom is toward the end. What's the obsession with sleeping arrangements, Riley? You know as well as I do it makes sense for Chad to move in with us until he and I graduate."

In addition to being Sean's sister, Riley had become one of Lauren's dearest friends over the past few years. Despite that fact, sometimes Lauren struggled with Riley's unusual view of the world and life in general.

"All I'm saying is, are you sure you don't want to share a room with Sean *and* Chad? Let's face it. You've got the hots for both of them. There's a lot of pent-up lust hovering in the air whenever the three of you get together. It's sort of stifling really."

Lauren sat down on a box, resting her elbows on her knees. "I'm committed to Sean, Riley. We've been together over two years. I'm not about to make a pass at his best friend."

Riley claimed the box next to her. "I'm not saying you should throw Sean over for Chad. Just add another man to the mix."

"Jesus. You know, we're not all as crazy as the Collins'. Most of us mere mortal beings just get through the days living normal lives, either alone or in pairs. Besides, I'm attending school to become a doctor. Of psychology. Not sure how living in a ménage would go over with my patients when I open a practice."

"I don't see anything weird about living in a threesome. Look at my brother Killian. He's been happily shacked up with Lily and Justin for years. I've always thought you, Sean and Chad were destined for the same."

Lauren shook her head. "Killian's deal is the exception, not the rule. I don't know of another person in the world living in that kind of setup."

"So that means no one else is? Pardon me, babe, but you don't know that many damn people. I bet there are loads of threesomes out there making it work."

"Why am I having this conversation with you? How do I let you drag me into stuff like this? The point is moot. I'm in love with Sean. We're eventually getting married and living happily ever after. The end."

Riley refused to be deterred. "And Chad?"

"Chad will hopefully be what he's always been. Our best friend. And God willing, he and I will achieve our dreams and open a practice together. This move hasn't changed anything except our address."

"I don't buy it."

Lauren rolled her eyes. "What don't you buy?"

"If you and Sean are so committed that you've decided to buy this house together and start shacking up, if this is just the first step toward marriage, then why bring Chad into the mix?"

"I'll admit the timing wasn't ideal, life-wise, but look at this house, Riley. It's gorgeous. Sean was helping Killian and Justin do some construction work on it so the former owner could sell. Sean took one look and knew it was our dream home. It's an easy commute to the pub for Sean and close to the university. When he brought me here to look at it, we knew we wanted it."

"It is beautiful. I guess I'm just worried you're both rushing things a bit."

Lauren sighed. She'd been feeling the same way lately. Sean hadn't exactly pushed her into buying the house, but he'd been so excited when he'd shown it to her. His enthusiasm had been infectious. Now that she was here, the reality of what she'd committed to was hitting her.

"Like I said, we weren't looking to buy a house until after I graduated in the spring. We couldn't leave Chad high and dry with just two more semesters to go. With Chad and me only working part-time while we finish grad school, having him rent the basement apartment helps us make the mortgage until I find a job. Besides, Chad couldn't afford the college apartment without a roommate, and while I know he wouldn't have minded advertising for one, it didn't seem fair to put him in that situation. He and Sean have lived together since high-school graduation."

"So this house-sharing deal is definitely a short-time thing?"

Lauren nodded. "Yep. Just until Chad and I earn our doctorates and find jobs."

Riley reached over and grasped Lauren's hand. "I'm really happy for you, Lauren."

Riley's words and her kind touch proved to be too much. Suddenly Lauren heard things falling from her lips that she hadn't meant to share. "When Sean brought me to see this house, he had a picnic basket with wine and bread and cheese. After taking me through the whole house, we sat on the floor in the living room. He pulled out the food, poured us some wine and told me he loved me and wanted to spend the rest of his life with me."

Riley laughed. "God, that's sappy. Sounds just like my baby brother."

"It was completely romantic. I looked at him and I knew. God, Riley, I knew all the way to my soul I wanted to live this lifetime with him."

"And now you are," Riley said.

Lauren looked down, tried to find a way to explain. "I made a choice. Part of being an adult means you have to make difficult decisions."

Riley's eyes narrowed. "You chose Sean."

"And I don't regret that. Not for a minute," Lauren interjected.

"But you still want Chad."

"I'm attracted to him. I'm close to him. I just think my

feelings for him are going to have to remain in the unrequited column."

"No," Riley said. "If you did that, you'd be lying to Sean, lying to yourself. Why would you let this relationship continue to grow with something like that overshadowing it? This is why the timing is right for you to do a little experimenting. I still say you should go for a threesome."

"No. Besides, even if Sean were onboard with the idea—"

Riley interrupted her. "You know Sean would go for it, don't you?"

Lauren shrugged noncommittally even though she knew her impulsive boyfriend was probably even more liberal-minded than his sister, who was currently attempting to push her into a ménage. Yes, she thought, Sean would definitely be open to the idea. She wasn't sure how she knew. It was just a feeling she got whenever she saw Chad and Sean together. They were closer than any two men she'd ever met. They shared everything, spent hours at a time together talking about everything and nothing. There had actually been a few occasions when she'd felt like an outsider in their relationship.

She also suspected Sean was aware of her attraction to Chad. Though he never overtly mentioned it, he'd definitely seen her checking Chad out on more than one occasion. Once he'd even winked at her as if to say "caught you".

Then she considered Chad and realized the idea was

impossible. "You told me yourself how upset Chad was when Lily hooked up with Justin and K. He was pissed off by the whole concept."

Riley considered her argument. "I don't know if he was pissed off by the ménage or the fact that it was his sister. Guys have pretty powerful protective instincts when it comes to sisters. Besides, he's obviously over it. He's always hanging around Lily and the guys."

"I think it's safe to say he's accepted it...for *her*, because it clearly makes her happy and Chad adores his sister. That doesn't mean he'll embrace it for himself. Besides, he's in the same boat I am. We're studying to become psychologists. I'm not sure living in a ménage would be good for any practice we might want to build."

Riley shrugged. "That's a lame excuse."

Lauren laughed. Trying to talk sense to Riley was always a waste of time. "A happy threesome is something only your family would try *and* succeed at. I'm just plain old Lauren Chase from Bethesda, Maryland. I think it's safe to say I better pack it in now while I'm ahead and enjoy my normal relationship with Sean."

"Never pegged you as someone to settle for safe."

Lauren narrowed her eyes. "I hardly call spending the rest of my life with your brother 'settling'. Sean's amazing, wonderful. He's everything I ever dreamed of in a man."

Riley leaned against the wall. "I have no doubt the two of you are well suited. But something's missing. Even I can see that, and you're forgetting something very important."

Lauren rose at the sound of feet climbing the stairs. "What's that?"

"One-*third*," Riley stressed the word, "of your happily ever after is a Collins. I think both of you will harbor a lifetime of regrets and what-ifs if you don't explore the idea before you get married. In fact, you probably should have done it before you bought the house."

Aaron appeared at the doorway. "Hiding out?"

Lauren was grateful for the man's timely interruption. Talking to Riley could sometimes be mentally exhausting.

Riley laughed at her husband's accusation as he walked over to them. "You know my aversion to anything resembling hard work. What do you think?"

Aaron rolled his eyes. "Just wanted to let you know Sean and Chad are looking for you, Lauren. Something about where to put the television. Lily's down there, fighting the good fight. She doesn't seem to think you'll like their living room setup."

"I better go put out the fire." She turned at the door in time to see Riley kissing Aaron on the cheek as he grabbed her ass. She grinned. "Thanks for the advice, Riley."

"Dear God," Aaron said, horrified. "You aren't taking Riley's advice on anything, are you?"

"Hey." Riley feigned offense. "I give amazing advice."

Lauren nodded. "You give insane, impossible advice, but I do appreciate your concern."

"You're not listening to it though, are you?" Riley asked.

Lauren shrugged and headed out the door.

"You know it's only as impossible as you make it, Lauren," Riley called out after her.

Riley's words drifted to her several times throughout that day...and the weeks that followed.

A MONTH LATER, all the boxes were emptied, the closets full of clothing, the kitchen full of food. The only thing still packed away was Lauren's true desires. And she was getting damn tired of it. Riley had planted a seed that had grown into a vine threatening to choke the life out of her.

The sound of Sean setting the kitchen table drifted down the hallway. Dinner was almost ready. She welcomed the idea of taking a break. She sure as hell wasn't accomplishing much right now.

She watched Chad read something off the computer screen, his face the picture of concentration. They'd spent hours...hell, *weeks* of their lives together like this, working on projects, debating a variety of subjects, dreaming about their shared career plans. They were so similar sometimes it was scary. They could finish each other's thoughts and there were times when she swore he could read her mind.

Chad rested his head on his hand, the pose drawing her attention to his muscular arm. Her imagination and lustful dreams of late were becoming more vivid with each replaying. Chad eating her pussy while she gave Sean a blowjob. Sean taking her from behind as she sucked on

Chad's cock. Chad and Sean both taking her—filling her ass and her pussy at the same time.

She rested her head against the back of her wingback chair and sighed, her mind filled with the latter image.

"Lousy book?"

She looked up to find Chad had turned in the desk chair and was looking at her. They'd both hit the office right after returning from class. Chad had set up his laptop and was working on a paper, while she was supposed to be studying for a test.

"What?" she asked.

"That's the third time in five minutes you've sighed. I figure either something you're reading is upsetting you or the book is boring."

She lifted the large textbook off her lap and flashed the cover at him.

He grinned. "Boring it is."

She hadn't read a single word since she'd come into the office and plopped down in the cushy chair in the corner. She had the same paper to write as Chad, but she was struggling to set her mind to it.

"Need help?" Chad offered.

She shook her head. The assignment wasn't difficult. "No, I understand it all. I just..." Her words faded away unfinished.

Chad frowned and rose. Crossing the room, he claimed the ottoman at her feet, his close proximity sending all the blood flowing to her hot spots—her nipples tightened and her pussy dampened. "You know, I'm starting to worry about you, Lauren. You haven't seemed like yourself since we moved into this house. Are you regretting your decision to let me bunk here? I know you and Sean were looking forward to setting up house. Don't wanna be in your way."

Damn psych majors, she thought. Chad was far too perceptive, too in tune with her emotions for her to hide anything for long. Only thing he seemed oblivious to was her desire to shove him to the floor and ride his cock until they both passed out. "Of course I don't regret you being here. I love living with you guys. I know I spent more time at yours and Sean's apartment over the past couple of years than I did at mine, but actually having the three of us under one roof full-time is fun. I'm sort of surprised how well everything's turned out."

Chad chuckled. "Yeah, me too. I mean, Sean and I have been roommates forever, but I have to admit I worried about changing the dynamics, adding you to the mix."

She gave him a hurt look and he quickly continued. "Don't look at me like that. I know we all get along, but you know how it is. You can be good friends with someone and still not be able to live with them. That's not true here. The three of us," he paused as if looking for the words, "we fit."

She nodded slowly, wondering exactly how well they would fit, say...on her bed. She cast the thought aside, afraid of giving herself away, and forced herself to answer lightly. "Yeah, I'd say, with the exception of the foosball table in the dining room, everything is pretty close to perfect."

Chad's eyes darkened. For just a moment she

wondered if he weren't hiding something too. Sometimes she got a feeling she wasn't the only one playing her cards close to her chest; that Chad and Sean were harboring some secrets as well. Unfortunately she couldn't figure out what those secrets might be. While Riley still swore Sean and Chad would be receptive to a threesome, neither of them gave her any indication they were unhappy with the status quo. She appeared to be the only horny one in the house, walking around with her mind in the gutter 24/7.

"Yeah," Chad said softly, "everything's perfect."

She narrowed her eyes, studying his face. His tone of voice betrayed his words and left her scrambling to figure out what he thought was off. "Chad," she started.

He covered his seriousness with a light laugh. "We'll move the foosball table eventually. Sean and I are getting close to finishing the basement. Once that's done, I'll take my stuff and the foosball table and give you both a bit more space."

Sean and Chad had worked wonders in the basement, creating the dream bachelor's pad complete with a small kitchen, living area, bedroom and its own outdoor entrance. Sean was pulling out all the stops, declaring that after Chad moved out it would become his man cave. The two spent ages plotting the future poker games and sporting-event parties they'd hold down there.

She gave him an annoyed look that was just for show. "You guys always say that and yet, that foosball table is still in my dining room. I swear I'm about to cover the damn thing with glass, throw a vase of flowers on it and call it my dining room table."

"That could work," Chad said. She tried to hide her surprise when he reached over and took her hands in his, the gesture out of character for him. While everyone within a twenty-mile radius could tell what Sean was feeling on any given day, Chad was more reserved and solitary. She was accustomed to Sean's continual, playful touches, but it was rare for Chad to touch her.

"You're sure you're okay with me living here?" he asked again.

She nodded.

"Good," he murmured. He leaned closer and for the briefest of moments, she thought he might kiss her. She didn't move, barely breathed, afraid to break the spell as his gaze held hers captive. What would it feel like to kiss him? She desperately wanted to find out.

She moved closer, a miniscule movement that Chad mimicked. She could smell cinnamon on his breath from the gum he'd been chewing earlier.

Her mouth watered for a taste and her eyes dropped to look at his lips, surprised to find he'd moved even closer.

"Hey, dinner's ready. I made spaghetti, and just so you know, clean up's gonna be a bitch." Sean entered the room. If he was suspicious of the way she and Chad quickly broke apart, standing up at the same time, he didn't give it away by his expression.

"Fuck, Sean. You made a mess on purpose, didn't you?" Chad accused, and Lauren was grateful for his quick reply. She scrambled to wipe away the thought that Chad had almost kissed her.

And she'd almost let him.

"Maybe," Sean joked. They'd instituted a rule when they first moved into the house that whoever cooked didn't have to clean. Sean, ever the prankster, had started making messes that had grown until recently it looked as if he'd used every dish they owned to make his meals.

Lauren crossed her arms over her chest, hoping to hide the fact her nipples were sharp enough to cut glass. She cleared her throat and forced a lightness to her voice. "You know, Chad, I'm thinking this need to make big messes in the kitchen is actually some sort of repressed emotion from Sean's childhood pushing its way to the surface."

Chad grinned at the joke. Sean hated when they tried to analyze him. "You could be right. Maybe the three of should sit down after dinner and discuss it. I'm sure I can find some research—"

Sean lifted his hands in surrender. "Oh hell no. None of that psychobabble bullshit. I'd rather clean up the mess myself than listen to any of that crap."

Lauren grabbed one of Sean's hands and shook it before making her way toward the kitchen. "Deal. Thanks."

She left the room quickly as Sean laughed. "No way. That wasn't an offer," he yelled behind her.

She claimed her spot at the table, refusing to look too hard at the piles of dishes on the counter and in the sink. He really had outdone himself this time.

Chad must've agreed because he muttered, "Jesus Christ," as he entered the kitchen and took his chair. Sean chuckled as he sat down and picked up the bottle of Boordy wine, pouring each of them a glass.

Lauren had to admit the food looked delicious and the table setting was gorgeous. Sean had even lit a candle. "Are we celebrating something?" she asked.

Sean nodded and lifted his glass, waiting until they followed suit. "Here's to one month of happy, relatively peaceful cohabitation."

They clinked glasses and laughed. Dinner passed quickly as they polished off the first bottle of wine and a good part of a second, the conversation light and lively. The three of them cleaned the kitchen together—Chad washing the dishes, Lauren drying and Sean putting them away.

After dinner, they watched a movie in the living room. Chad relaxed in the recliner while she and Sean cuddled on the couch. Lauren tried to remember when she'd spent a more peaceful evening and realized there'd been a hundred nights just as perfect—all of them spent like this, with Sean and Chad.

"Guess I should head to bed. I have an early class tomorrow," she said, standing and stretching.

Sean yawned. "Yeah, I won't be too far behind you. I'm helping K at the construction site early tomorrow then I'm covering the lunch shift for Ewan while he takes Natalie to the baby doctor. And tomorrow night is my night to man the bar at the pub. I'm tired just thinking about it."

Lauren knew Sean's grumbling was all for show. She'd never known a man more devoted to his family. There was, quite simply, nothing he wouldn't do for his pop or his brothers and sisters. She wished she had a similarly close relationship with her brother. Though she loved him dearly, they rarely saw each other as real life constantly seemed to get in the way.

"Jeez," Chad said, still reclining. "I don't know how the hell you keep all those nieces and nephews straight."

Sean laughed. "There are only five rugrats, six if you count Ewan's soon-to-be-here baby."

"Six," Chad repeated, shaking his head as if trying to wrap his mind around the large number.

"I think you're forgetting Sean is one of seven," Lauren added. "The Collins family is used to lots of kids and noise and activity. You and I are products of the boring two-kid family concept."

"My mom always said she'd had one boy and one girl and there wasn't anything else to go for so she was done." Chad put his hands behind his head.

Sean laughed. "She could've tried for twins."

Chad shuddered. "Twins is no joke. I'm not sure how your brother Tristan manages with those two rowdy toddlers of his."

Sean shrugged. "Tris was a twin. Believe me, besides Killian, there's no one else in my family better suited to raise twin hellions than him."

"I think you could do it," Lauren said, imagining Sean

as a father. He was good-natured, fun, easygoing and she had no doubt he'd be an amazing dad.

"I'm looking forward to getting the chance."

Though the two of them had talked often about their future together, they'd never discussed the idea of having kids. Right now she was too focused on her career plans to see beyond getting a degree and opening a practice.

Then she realized Sean's comment made sense. His future was settled. He had earned his four-year degree and he had a job he loved. Sean had gone to college simply to appease his sister Keira and his pop. They'd both wanted him to get a degree. However, Sean had known from the time he was a kid, his dream was to work at the pub. He'd told Lauren more than once the pub was as close to heaven on earth as he'd ever found and he didn't intend to leave it until they carried him out in a box.

Now Sean had bought this house with her, the two of them moving that much closer to forever. Once again, she felt a slight sense of unease. For the most part, their future *had* begun, so they should be thinking about the next step —marriage and family.

Chad groaned. "Twins? You gotta be kidding me. The idea of one kid terrifies me."

"Really?" Sean asked. "Why?"

Lauren perched on the end of the coffee table, all thoughts of bed gone as she waited for Chad's answer.

Chad studied Sean's face for a long time before responding, the two of them sharing a look Lauren couldn't begin to understand. "I can't even sort out my own fucked-up life. How could I expect to raise a kid with any level of success?"

Lauren was confused by his answer. "Your life isn't fucked-up."

Chad snorted. "Sure it is."

Lauren looked at Sean, expecting him to jump into the conversation, offer her some help in refuting Chad's words, but he fell silent. Once again, she sensed some underlying current she wasn't privy to. This wasn't the first time she'd gotten a feeling Sean knew something about Chad that he wasn't sharing. In the past, she'd let it slide. Tonight, it was rubbing against the grain.

Sean stood hastily. "Doesn't matter anyway. Not like any of us are having kids right away. I'm heading up for the night. You coming, Lauren?"

She nodded slowly, trying to decide if it was smart to let the conversation end. She looked toward the recliner just in time to see the briefest flash of pain cross Chad's face before it disappeared once again. He'd shut down and she knew he wouldn't discuss his unusual comment any further.

"How about you?" she asked. "You have an early class too."

Chad closed his eyes. "I'm gonna hang out down here for a little while. I'll see you guys in the morning."

She silently followed Sean upstairs. Maybe tonight hadn't been as perfect as she'd thought.

CHAPTER TWO

Chad finished nailing the last piece of drywall, then stepped back to survey his work. He ran the back of his forearm along his sweaty forehead, trying the capture his perspiration before it rolled into his eyes. He could hear Sean cutting another two-by-four behind him. It was Sunday—they only day they had to work on his basement apartment. Between Chad's classes and grading papers for the course he was teaching to help pay for tuition, and Sean working two jobs, they'd be lucky to finish this damn apartment by the year 2050. They'd been hard at work since dawn and it was just about time to break for lunch.

He glanced around the space that would eventually be his temporary home—and felt the same dull ache in his gut that hit whenever he remembered the fact Sean and Lauren would be building a future in this house without him.

He pictured Lauren's face as she'd looked earlier this

week in the office. She'd seemed so sad, he'd felt compelled to kiss her. If Sean hadn't walked in when he did, he would have.

He'd nearly kissed his best friend's girl. The guilt he'd suffered since that near miss returned full-force. Worst part was, the guilt wasn't based on the fact he'd tried to kiss her so much as on the fact he really, *really* wanted to try again. He licked his lips and imagined placing his mouth on Lauren's.

He was going straight to hell. He felt like the loser in that old Rick Springfield song, constantly wishing for Jessie's girl—or in his case, Sean's.

Of course, he couldn't blame Lauren for choosing Sean over him. Sean was a natural with women. He'd inherited his good looks and large build from his father, sharing the same dark hair and eyes the other Collins brothers possessed. He had a personality people flocked too—quick-witted, easygoing, the perfect combination of cynical and nice.

What did Chad have to offer Lauren in return? He was too serious, too boring. He barely topped six feet, and while Sean was a natural at the social scene, Chad preferred being alone or, at the most, alone with just Sean and Lauren. He hated crowds, hated making small talk and, as he glanced at Sean's smug morning-after face, he realized he hated listening to Sean make love to *his* dream girl.

"Shit," Sean muttered, working out a kink in his neck

as he stood. "Didn't realize this project was gonna take so fucking long."

"Can't make much progress when the two of us only have time to work on it on Sundays."

Sean put his hands on his hips and looked at what they'd accomplished that morning. He'd taken his shirt off an hour earlier and Chad couldn't help but admire his friend's physique. Sean was a man's man, like the rest of his crazy brothers. They worked with their hands as well as their minds and it showed. Since taking on the part-time construction job with his older brother Killian, Sean's form had hardened, become more defined, his skin turning a golden tan.

He stared at his best friend's muscular body and felt his cock stir slightly.

Fuck! As if it wasn't bad enough he was lusting over Sean's girlfriend, now he was getting a hard-on looking at *Sean*. Chad forced the thought away, something he'd gotten very adept at over the years. There was no way in hell he was going down that road.

He quickly averted his gaze, looking down at his own body. Chad felt like a middle-aged accountant whenever he stood next to Sean. He spent too much time indoors. While he was trim, no one would call him built. He certainly wasn't sporting a six-pack. Shit. He'd be lucky to find just one in his pack and his skin was too pale from lack of sun.

"Jeez. We've still got a shitload of work to do down

here," Sean muttered, running a hand through his hair, leaving a few pieces of sawdust clinging in its wake.

Chad nodded. "Yeah. We do. Is that a problem? I could always rent a room somewhere if you want me out of your way upstairs." Chad tried not to look too hopeful, but Sean giving him the boot sure would make his life a lot easier. He hadn't been sleeping well lately, his hot fantasies keeping him up well after lights out.

"Are you kidding me? Hell no, man. Things are working out great."

Chad nodded slowly. Great wasn't a word he'd use to describe the current hell he was residing in, but he wasn't about to burst Sean's bubble. His best friend had a habit of focusing on the positive and ignoring the negative. In the past, Chad had viewed that personality trait as either admirable or annoying as fuck, depending on the day. Today, it was irritating him worse than a rock in his shoe. His hand was calloused and his dick was chafed from whacking off so much lately. He needed to find a girl-friend...soon.

Unfortunately, every woman he dated ended up being compared to Lauren. Every one of them came up lacking and he usually went home alone.

"You guys ready for some lunch?"

Chad glanced up and found Lauren coming down the stairs with a plate full of sandwiches and a bag of chips under her arm. She was wearing her Sunday outfit, a comfy pair of lounge pants and a loose tee. Her auburn hair was pulled up in a ponytail again. His fingers itched to pull her hair down. He wanted to run his fingers through it and catch a whiff of the scent of her coconut shampoo. That scent alone never failed to drive his arousal up an extra notch, the smell his favorite part of carpooling with her to early morning classes. Of course, he then spent the rides trying to shield an erection.

Jesus. He needed psychological help and the words "Physician, heal thyself" floated through his mind.

"Hot damn, baby. You showed up just in the nick of time," Sean said, grabbing the plate and setting it down on a board lying atop two sawhorses. "I'm starving."

Lauren laughed and pointed at the plate. "Two peanut butter and banana ones for you," she said to Sean. "I keep waiting for the day you'll outgrow that, you know."

Sean shook his head. "Never gonna happen. They're my Sunday specials."

Chad grinned at the remark. Sean's mother, Sunday, had packed the sandwiches in Sean's lunch every single day when they were in elementary school. Chad recalled the lump he'd gotten in his throat the first day Sean returned to school after Sunday's death from cancer. They'd been in fourth grade. For the first time in his life, Sean stood in line to buy the cafeteria lunch. The next day, Sean's sister Keira had picked up the routine and Sean was back to peanut butter and banana sandwiches, but Chad remembered realizing at that moment exactly how much his best friend had lost.

"And there's tuna on rye for you, Chad."

Chad grinned, pleased that she knew his favorite sandwich as well.

"I'll go back up and grab the sodas," Lauren said. "Couldn't get it all down here in one trip."

"No worries," Sean said, passing her before she made it to the bottom step. "I need to wash my hands and grab a couple more tools from the garage. I'll bring them down with me."

"Cool," Lauren said and they watched as Sean took the stairs two at a time, reaching the top in record speed.

"Never seen anyone who always lives life in fast forward. Guy runs everywhere." Chad's observation was meant to be a joke but Lauren nodded, picking up the subject as a serious one.

"I know. I've always wondered about that. Sometimes I think he's just impatient, but it doesn't fit. Of course, neither does the alternative."

"The alternative?" Chad asked.

"Maybe he's trying to outrun something."

Chad considered her comment, unsure how to respond. Until she'd mentioned it, he'd never really thought much about Sean's need for perpetual motion. Now he thought maybe she was right. He tried to pinpoint when Sean had become a whirlwind of activity. Chad knew for a fact he hadn't always been that way. In high school, Sean was laid back, a slow-and-steady kind of guy.

No, the change had definitely occurred in college. He'd begun to take on more chores; attended five classes per semester at the university while working part-time at the bar. It wasn't unusual for Sean to be out of their apartment six or seven days a week, only stopping in for showers and sleep.

After graduation, Chad had expected Sean to settle down, but then he took on the part-time job at the construction company and his days were still filled with constant movement.

A niggling worry crept in about what—or who—Sean was trying to outrun. Chad pushed the idea aside. He wasn't going there...not even in his own thoughts. "I think you're overanalyzing, doctor." His lighthearted tease had the desired affect and Lauren dropped the subject.

"You guys are making some awesome progress down here. It's really starting to look like an apartment," Lauren said, walking around and surveying their work.

Chad scoffed. "That's funny. Sean and I were just bitching about how much we still have left to do."

"Oh no. I don't think it will take you much longer. Have you decided what color you're painting the walls? What pictures to hang? Where the furniture goes?"

Chad laughed. "I think I'll leave that to you. I don't mind building the wall, but God help me if I know what to put on it once it's there."

Lauren snickered. "Well, then, I know just the thing. We'll start with a pale rose color in here." She gestured around her as she spoke. "This is the bedroom, right?"

He nodded and restrained a grin at her teasing. "Rose? Really? I was thinking purple or maybe a rainbow design."

"Oh wow. That would rock. Then we can get a floral bedspread and a lot of throw pillows."

He put his hands on his hips and pretended to take her seriously. "Throw pillows are a definite. Maybe scatter a bunch of scented candles around."

"Yes," she said, laughing. "I have some lilac-scented ones that are to die for."

He shook his head. "Not lilac. Coconut."

She looked at him strangely, but shrugged and said, "Okay, coconut.

"We'll put a giant mirror over your bed here," she continued. Lauren took a step closer to him, pointing to the wall he'd just finished building between what would eventually be his bedroom and the living area. She tripped on the hammer he'd carelessly left on the floor. Reaching out, he caught her before she could do a faceplant on rough wooden floorboards.

Helping her catch her balance with his hands on her middle, he tried to ignore how close she was, the narrowness of her waist.

"Shit. Thanks," she said, looking at him, her face inches from his. "Damn clumsiness."

He shook his head, not able to make himself release his hold on her. "I shouldn't have left the hammer there. You could've hurt yourself."

"That's okay." Her words suddenly sounded breathless and Chad imagined her speaking with the same tone as he pushed his cock into her tight, wet warmth.

He closed his eyes, savoring the image, unsure exactly

when he'd leaned closer. His lips glanced against hers and his eyes flew open. Lauren's face was a perfect combination of surprise and naked desire. He grasped onto the desire aspect and deepened his kiss. He held her tighter, opening his mouth to brush his tongue against hers. He'd been dying to taste her for years and she was just as sweet as he'd imagined.

For the briefest of moments she returned his kiss and Chad realized she truly was the woman of his heart. Then she pushed away, her face flushed, her breathing labored.

She shook her head and he realized he was the biggest fool on earth.

"No."

"I'm sorry," he said quickly.

She placed her fingers on her lips and Chad wished he could turn back time. Rewind the last two minutes to take the look of despair out of her beautiful green eyes.

"I shouldn't have done that."

"Why did you?" she asked.

He grinned sadly at her question. Lauren was a born psychologist. She was probably freaking out about him kissing her, but rather than run or rail, she hit him with the twenty-dollar question.

"I don't know." It was a cop-out and a lie. He knew why. He studied her face and realized she knew too.

Footsteps on the stairs had them moving farther apart. Sean juggled three glasses filled with ice and soda, oblivious to the charged atmosphere in the basement. He put the drinks next to the sandwiches and pulled a small level and some pliers out of his back pocket. "Remind me to unpack all the shit still in boxes in the garage. Took me ages to find a damn pair of pliers. Oh, and we only have Diet Dr. Pepper left in the fridge. We're gonna have to run to the store," Sean complained.

Lauren smiled. Chad marveled at how easily she managed to find her composure. "I love Diet Dr. Pepper. I was just telling Chad how impressed I am with how much you've done today. The place is really starting to come together."

"Yeah," Sean said easily. "I think it's gonna turn out cool. Just a bitch trying to get it done in bits and pieces. I need to take a week off from work and just go after it. When's your fall break, Chad? I was thinking I'd ask for some time then. We could knock a shitload of this off in a week."

Chad nodded. "My next break is the week of Thanksgiving. We'll tackle it then."

"Cool. I'll talk to Tris and see what we can work out on the schedule for the pub." Sean grabbed a sandwich and started eating. He'd just swallowed the first bite when his cell phone rang. "Speak of the devil," he said, glancing at the phone.

As Sean answered the phone and started talking to his brother, Chad could hear his friend making plans to head over to Tristan's house to watch the football game later.

Lauren turned to look at him. "Don't go to Tristan's house. We'll talk later," she whispered, and Chad watched her climb the stairs.

Fuck. Later. What did that mean? Knowing Lauren, it wouldn't be good.

—

CHAD SPRAWLED out on his bed, tossing the book he'd been unsuccessfully reading onto the mattress next to him. He'd turned down Sean's invite to watch the game, claiming he had a headache. Rubbing his brow, he realized that wasn't too far away from the truth. He'd stressed over the kiss he'd shared with Lauren until he thought his head was about to explode. He'd started to seek her out several times throughout the afternoon, but he couldn't figure out what the hell to say.

He'd already apologized, though he suspected she didn't know exactly what he was sorry about. He wasn't regretting the kiss. He'd wanted to taste her lips for far too long. But he hadn't wanted to hurt her or Sean, and with his impulsive action, he knew he had.

He closed his eyes, his mind drifting back to the morning when Lauren and Sean had told him about the changed dynamic of their relationship.

His parents had been in town visiting and he'd planned to spend the night at Lily's place. However, the idea of spending the night on her lumpy couch when his comfortable bed was just a few miles away seemed stupid, so he'd said his goodbyes and headed home...

AS HE WALKED into the apartment, he heard voices drifting down the hallway from Sean's room. Curious, he walked toward the sounds, only realizing as he stood outside the door that Sean was having sex with someone. He grinned and rolled his eyes. Sean was obviously bringing his A game if the woman's cries were anything to judge by. He chuckled and started to walk to his room—then he recognized Lauren's voice.

Stunned, he stood in the empty hallway until he heard Sean and Lauren climaxing. His cock twitched. Feeling like the world's biggest pervert, he quickly walked away, shutting himself up in his room and praying all night he'd misunderstood, misheard. He knew he hadn't.

The next morning as he poured a cup of coffee, Sean and Lauren walked into the kitchen together.

"Hey," Sean said rather sheepishly.

Chad nodded. "Hey."

Lauren looked uncomfortable, though adorable in Sean's T-shirt and sweatpants. "Thought you were out for the night," she said.

He shrugged. "Change of plans."

"Listen, man..." Sean started.

Chad held up his hand. He couldn't remain in this room, couldn't have this conversation. "I got it, Sean. Figured it out all by myself. Congratulations. You two make an awesome couple."

Lauren frowned slightly, clearly uncertain of his sincerity. "You really think so?"

He nodded and eyed the exit. At the moment, both of his friends were blocking it. "Been a long time coming."

While Lauren breathed an obvious sigh of relief and smiled at him, Sean didn't appear to accept his words as easily. "You're sure you're okay with this?" he asked.

Chad snorted, wondering where he was finding the ability to lie so well. "Me? Why the hell wouldn't I be? It's great. Terrific. Listen, I gotta head back to Lily's. One of the conditions of my coming home last night was a promise I'd be back in time for breakfast. I'm supposed to be helping her entertain my folks."

Sean smiled and walked toward him. Chad knew his friend was coming to give him a friendly pat on the arm, but if Sean touched him, he'd fall apart. He skirted around Sean rapidly, lightly bumping into Lauren in his haste to escape the kitchen.

So much for his Academy Award-winning performance. He'd tipped his hand. Given himself away.

"Chad," Sean started, but Chad had cleared the doorway. Freedom was within his grasp.

"Catch you two later," he said, grabbing his car keys and opening the front door.

"Dammit, Chad..." Sean called.

Chad turned to see his best friend standing right behind him. A quick glance over Sean's shoulder proved Lauren hadn't followed him. She had remained in the kitchen.

"What?"

Sean looked worried. "Are you really okay with this?"

Chad scowled. "What if I wasn't, Sean? What if I said I fucking hated this? What would you do?"

Sean didn't reply. He didn't have to. Chad could see the utter devastation in his best friend's face at the thought of having to choose between their friendship and his new girlfriend.

Chad couldn't stand the look, couldn't let his best friend hurt. "I don't hate it. You surprised me, that's all. Give me a few days to get used to the idea."

Sean studied his face and Chad fought hard to keep it impassive.

"I love her," Sean whispered.

So do I.

Chad didn't speak the words. Instead, he placed a friendly hand on Sean's shoulder and spoke the words written on his heart. "I'm happy for you." He was. Sean was a great guy and he deserved a loving, beautiful woman like Lauren. "But I'm telling you right now, if you ask one of your brothers to be best man at your wedding instead of me, I'm kicking your ass."

Sean laughed and the tension passed. "That position has been yours since kindergarten, man. No worries."

"Great." Chad forced a smile then nodded toward the kitchen. "Sounds like you two worked up a bit of an appetite last night. You better go feed the girl."

Sean laughed. "I will. You coming home later?"

Chad shook his head. He needed time away from here. The family get-together he'd been happy to escape last night was suddenly looking pretty good. "Naw. I don't think Lily's gonna let me out of another night of bonding with our parents. Besides, I'm not in the mood to listen to you and Lauren go at it like fucking rabbits."

Sean grinned and Chad braced himself for his friend's bragging. Hell, he'd invited it with his stupid rabbit comment, had let Sean think he'd be able to stomach listening to him talk about sleeping with Lauren. He was surprised by Sean's words.

"Thanks," Sean said quietly.

Chad blinked twice, saw the sincerity in his friend's face. He nodded. "Bye, Sean."

Sean lifted his hand. "Later."

Chad walked out and considered their parting remarks. Chad felt as if he was saying goodbye to his best friend, as well as Lauren. Things were changing. Nothing would ever be the same again.

CHAD RUBBED his eyes wearily as he considered how much had changed—and how much had stayed the same— since that morning. He was still in love with his best friend's girl and there still wasn't anything he wouldn't sacrifice to ensure Sean's happiness.

"Hey." Lauren's voice sounded in the doorway.

He pushed to a sitting position. He wasn't surprised she'd come to him. While he was acting like a coward, Lauren was nothing if not forthright. She would never beat around the bush if she thought there was an issue that needed to be resolved.

"Hey," he echoed.

She didn't move to come into his bedroom and he tried to fight off his annoyance at that fact. He didn't blame her for keeping her distance, but it still hurt.

"I'm not mad," she said quickly.

He frowned at her comment. He'd never thought she was. "I know. I'm glad. I meant what I said earlier, Lauren. I'm sorry I kissed you. I was out of line. I'd never try to fuck up what you and Sean have. Just sort of lost my head there for a minute."

She took a couple steps into the room, nodding. "You weren't the only one, but it can't happen again. I'm in love with Sean."

His heart broke at her admission even though he'd known that truth for years. "I know."

"I want to tell him about the kiss."

Chad looked at her and knew in an instant she was serious. He also knew she wouldn't say a word to Sean if he asked her to keep it a secret.

Before he could reply, she continued, "I plan to spend the rest of my life with him. I don't ever want lies or secrets in our relationship. Not ever. That's no way to live a life."

She was right. Chad knew it. "I'll tell him."

She shook her head but he refused to take no for an answer. "I initiated the kiss, Lauren. I'm going to be the one to tell him. If he gets pissed off and decides to take a swing, I'm gonna be the one standing there to take it."

"Sean would never hit me *or* you, and you know it."

Chad nodded, knowing her words were true. "I sort of hope he does."

She grinned and rolled her eyes. "Is this the guy form of penance? You mess up so you take a punch?"

He shrugged, her words provoking an old memory. He closed his eyes to block out the last time he and Sean had taken punches at each other. "Yeah, something like that."

A car pulled into the driveway and they both stared at each other.

She took a deep breath and he could see a slight tremble in her hands. Great. He'd really fucked this one up. If Sean dumped her over his fucking mistake, Chad would be the one throwing punches, making sure his best friend didn't lose the best thing in his life. They'd make their confession and then Chad would come upstairs, pack his shit and get out of here. Maybe Lily would let him bunk at her place.

The thought brought him more relief than he would have expected. Had he kissed Lauren as a way of screwing things up so he could escape this house? He looked at her beautiful face...

No. He'd kissed her because he was in love with her. Plain and simple.

The front door opened and Sean's voice boomed from the floor below. "Where is everybody?"

Lauren turned toward the hallway. "I'll go with you."

He wanted to insist she remain upstairs, but he knew she wouldn't listen. "Fine." He rose from his bed and passed her, Lauren on his heels. Sean was in the living room when they got downstairs.

"Hey," he said with a big grin. "Ravens fucking kicked ass. Did you catch the game?"

Chad shook his head. "No. I had some reading to do for my class tomorrow." It wasn't a lie. He *still* had the reading to do as he hadn't been able to concentrate on the words on the page all afternoon.

"Damn, man. You better make a good paycheck as a psychologist. Can't imagine any job worth missing a football game."

Lauren laughed, but Chad detected the strain in her voice. She was nervous.

No need to prolong the agony.

"I kissed Lauren this afternoon."

The words flew from his lips more abruptly than he'd intended.

Sean stared at him for a very long, very frozen moment. Then his gaze traveled to Lauren. "He did?"

From the corner of his eyes, Chad saw Lauren nod.

"It was my fault," he added. "She tripped and I caught her. It was a stupid, impulsive thing to do, but I swear to you, man, it'll never happen again."

Sean rubbed his cheek and Chad stood his ground. It was impossible to know how Sean would respond to anything. Typically his reactions were so unconventional, they left Chad speechless.

This time was no exception.

"You've never kissed her before today?" Sean asked.

Chad shook his head, confused.

Sean looked at Lauren then winked. "Is he a better kisser than me?"

She released a loud breath that betrayed how much confessing to Sean had scared her. Leave it to his friend to break the tension with humor. "Sean," she said.

Sean shrugged. "Sort of surprised it's never happened before this. I mean, you guys have been in each other's faces pretty much night and day for the past six years."

Chad put his hands in his pockets, unsure how to reply. Sean was right. He'd lusted after Lauren for years. Spent at least a thousand nights dreaming of her soft lips...

He needed to get out of here. He wasn't sure how to explain the difference between living in this house versus the apartment he'd shared with Sean, but it was as if his entire life was suddenly moving too fast, as if his days were numbered.

Sean and Lauren would get married, move on without him, and he was acting like an ass trying to cling to something that wasn't there to begin with.

He sighed. It felt as if a huge part of his life was missing.

"You don't wanna take a swing at me?" Chad asked. "I think if the shoe was on the other foot, I'd pound your ass into the ground."

Sean shook his head. "I'm not mad."

Chad looked at Lauren, who grinned as they both recalled her saying the exact same words a few minutes earlier.

Sean sat down on the couch. "I guess I should be, but I'm not. In fact..." He paused and Chad waited to hear the rest of his sentence.

"In fact what?" Lauren asked.

Sean grinned crookedly. "Naw, it'll sound too weird."

"Say it," Lauren prompted.

"I'm sort of sorry I didn't get to see it."

"What the fuck is wrong with you?" Chad asked, his temper exploding. He'd been kicking his own ass all afternoon, feeling like the world's biggest shit, and now Sean was saying he was sorry he didn't get to see his best friend betraying him.

"Told you it was weird."

Lauren perched herself on the end of the recliner. "Only *you* would regret something like that." She laughed lightly before sobering. "Sean, I love you. I would never, ever cheat on you. I swear it."

"I know that. And I think if it had been any other guy doing the kissing, you'd be pulling me off him right now as I tried to beat him to a pulp." Sean looked at him and Chad fought to catch a breath at the complete and unquestionable understanding in his friend's gaze. "But Chad's different. He's a part of us."

Sean's words hit him like a blow to the chest and Chad realized two things. One, he *wanted* to be a part of them. And two—he wasn't.

"I'll pack," he said. "Move out."

"What?" Sean stood quickly, shaking his head. "The

hell you will. Didn't you hear what I said? You belong here." Sean looked at Lauren. "Right?"

Clearly Sean was suddenly worried Lauren would be uncomfortable with the current living arrangements.

"Right," she said, so confidently there could be no mistaking her agreement.

They both wanted him to stay. He'd never felt so wanted...and so trapped.

CHAPTER THREE

Sean kicked back on the couch, his bare feet resting on the coffee table in front of him as he watched a repeat of *That '70s Show*. He popped another Oreo, not finding much comfort in the snack. Cookies had always been his no-fail pick-me-up. Today the sweet treat was falling short. It was Friday and he was grateful to see the longest week of his life finally end. Usually he worked at the pub, but he'd begged off for the night, promising Killian he'd work an extra day next week if he'd cover his shift.

This had been the only time all week he'd been completely alone and he needed that time to get his thoughts in order.

He looked around his new living room. Sean wondered if he hadn't jumped out of the frying pan and into the fire by initiating this new living arrangement.

He'd wanted Lauren since he'd first laid eyes on her during their freshman year in college. He couldn't imagine a day where he wouldn't want her as fiercely as he wanted her now. Sex with her not only sated his desires, but kept him coming back for more. However, this week he'd begun to sense her pulling away, holding him at arm's length.

It was obviously because of the kiss with Chad. He'd tried everything he knew to set her mind at ease, assure her he wasn't angry, but he'd started to suspect it wasn't guilt driving her actions. Maybe that kiss hadn't been impulsive or just a fluke.

No. It was clearly the wrench in the clockwork of Sean's life—Chad. Having his best friend move into the house he bought to share with Lauren was seriously fucking with his head...and his libido. He took a calming breath and for the seven-gazillionth time, pushed that unwelcome thought from his mind. His pop always used to tell him the heart wants what it wants. What his dear father had forgotten to add was that sometimes the heart *couldn't* have what it wanted, no matter what.

He closed his eyes and imagined Chad kissing Lauren. Ever since they'd confessed, he'd had a terrible time trying to erase the picture from his mind. What kind of kiss was it? Open-mouthed? With tongue? Was it a light, soft, gentle exploration or a passionate, set-the-house-on-fire embrace? He'd allowed every example to play over and over in his mind, and he stood by what he'd said the night they confessed. He wished he'd been there to see it.

Chad and Lauren were in class until six. He glanced at the clock on the DVR and sighed when he heard footsteps on the porch.

Time's up.

As if on cue, the front door opened and he grinned when he heard Lauren talking to Chad. She could talk the paint off the walls. He loved her constant chatter.

"All I'm saying is, I don't think Professor Webster wants us to copy a bunch of information out of a textbook. In fact, he said those exact words."

Chad shrugged. "If he wanted decent research he should have let us pick topics that interest us. Who the hell makes you draw them out of a hat? It's bullshit. He's getting fuck-all from me."

Sean lowered his feet to the floor as they walked into the living room.

Lauren rolled her eyes, obviously frustrated. "The randomness fits. We sure as hell can't pick and choose our patients when we open our practice. It makes sense that we might have to research things that make us uncomfortable. That's sort of the point of the whole project."

"Rough class?" Sean asked.

Chad walked over to turn on the lamp on the end table. Dusk was kicking in. It was only late October, but Sean couldn't wait for spring to hit already. He was sick of darkness descending so early and ready for the long, lively days of summer.

Lauren shook her head. "Not rough. The class is actually really interesting."

Chad snorted. "Lauren's been looking forward to Human Sexuality since our freshmen year. Makes me think she's a nympho."

Sean laughed while Lauren punched Chad playfully on the arm. Chad wrapped his arm around her neck and playfully messed up her hair as she struggled to free herself. Sean watched them wrestle and felt the usual pang that hit whenever he watched Chad and Lauren together. The emotion was one he couldn't put a name to, though he'd given it some thought. It wasn't jealousy, it was just...

He didn't know what it was. Sometimes he thought Chad and Lauren's shared ambitions made them more compatible than he and Lauren. Now that he knew Chad was just as interested in her, things had definitely changed.

Yep, they were all knee-deep in a triangle and he was certain Lauren and Chad didn't realize just how twisted.

"Don't you wish you knew for sure," she teased.

Sean put his feet back on the coffee table and chuckled, relieved they were finally acting like normal again. The past week had been awkward. Sean was anxious to have his friends back. "I can answer that question. Yes. She is. So what are you two fighting about?"

"Professor Webster gave us a big assignment. Huge project that'll take us the rest of the damn semester to research." Lauren dropped down on the other end of the couch and started pulling off her shoes, tossing them aside. "Oh my God, I'm tired. Friday's suck."

"They're not so bad. So what's the assignment? I can't imagine anything in a human sexuality class could be that bad. Anything I can help you research?"

He gave Lauren a wicked look and she laughed. "Not unless you feel like donning leather and wielding a whip."

Sean struggled to catch his breath at her words, the comment striking too close to the vein of a secret desire pulsating through him.

Chad chuckled and interrupted his thoughts before they could travel too far down that horny lane. "Jesus, Lauren. It's a freaking research paper. Just Google your topic and be done with it."

Lauren shook her head. "That's not good enough, Chad, and you know it. This project is sixty percent of our grade. Professor Webster said you needed to put yourself in the mindset."

"Mindset?" Sean asked.

Lauren looked at him. "The topics were all different types of sexual preferences, fetishes, that kind of thing. Our assignment is to delve into our subject." She turned to Chad. "We have to put ourselves in the shoes of a person who walks around in that skin all the time and analyze the psychology behind it."

"Great. More analyzing." Sean's tone showed his annoyance. "FYI, right now. I'm not gonna be the guinea pig on this project. You two have poked at my psyche so much these last few years, it's a wonder I haven't broken under the mental stress."

"Ha ha." Lauren dug a hair band out of her jeans pocket and pulled her long auburn hair into a ponytail. "Your psyche is just fine, Sean. One of the reasons why you suck for the experiments. You're too grounded, too well-adjusted."

"Come from hardy stock," Sean teased, imitating his

pop. "We Collins men are well known for our masculine—"

"Oh God," Chad interrupted. "Here we go with the Collins creed again. Leave that speech to your pop. He does it better."

Chad started rummaging around the room for the remote.

Sean pulled it out from where it was tucked into the cushion next to him and waved it at Chad, then chuckled. "I'll tell him you said so tomorrow at work." He put the remote behind his back when his friend reached for it.

"My turn," Chad said, his hand outstretched.

"Nope. Not watching the news. It's always bad. I prefer the beauty of a mindless sitcom."

Chad scowled. "You know, I didn't have to ask. I could just take it from you."

Sean beckoned him closer with a *bring it* gesture. Chad took a step toward the couch but Lauren interrupted them before the usual wrestling match could ensue.

"Jesus. Do the words *grow up* mean anything to you two?" Lauren leaned against the arm of the couch, resting her feet in Sean's lap and wiggling her toes. Chad backed off and Sean reached down to rub Lauren's feet. "Ah, bliss. A Sean Collins foot rub."

He rubbed harder, in the way he knew she liked, as she shifted slightly. He tightened his grip on her feet lest she accidentally brush against his suddenly erect cock. He couldn't touch her without rising to the occasion.

Lauren sighed. "I can't think with all that noise

anyway. It's not like you guys ever really watch it unless it's sports. Give me the remote."

Sean stopped his ministrations to hand it over and Lauren turned the television off completely.

Chad started to protest but Lauren ignored him, picking up their previous conversation. "We can't poke into your mind, Sean, because I just told you, for this project, Chad and I have to delve into our own psyches."

Sean glanced over at Chad and gave him a shit-eating grin. "That should be fun to watch."

Lauren smirked at him. "Yeah well, neither one of us is too thrilled about the subject matter we drew."

"It's a stupid fucking project." Chad plopped down on the recliner across the room and Sean studied his angry face. Chad rarely lost his cool, never showed much emotion, unlike Sean, who lived his life with his heart on his sleeve—another Collins trait.

Sometimes it amazed him how long their friendship had persevered. Chad was serious, while Sean preferred to address everything in life with humor. Chad was a thinker while Sean lived on impulse and yet, despite their opposite natures, it worked.

Sean turned to Lauren. "What topic did you pick out of the hat?"

She blushed. Sean almost did a double take at the sight. While Chad was typically calm, Lauren was unflappable. Nothing fazed her. Now, in less than five minutes, he'd witnessed Chad's anger and seen an embarrassed Lauren. What the hell was this project about?

Chad smirked. "Tell him, Lauren. Tell him what mindset you're gonna have to get into."

Lauren shot their friend a dirty look, and then she looked at Sean. "I pulled submissiveness out of the hat."

Sean laughed loudly. "No way. That should be good." Lauren was as submissive as Attila the Hun.

She narrowed her eyes. "Very funny. You know, despite what you guys think, I'm perfectly capable of acing this assignment. I'm open-minded, completely able to relate to all different sorts of people, I adapt easily. While this wouldn't have been my first choice—"

"Or second or third or twelfth," Sean added with a grin.

Lauren nodded in agreement. "Even so, this will be no problem."

Sean nodded, but he was sure his face was betraying his true thoughts. She was independent and strong-willed, firmly in control of her own destiny. He was fairly certain Lauren wouldn't have a clue how to follow someone else's lead, how to allow someone to call the shots for her, and he wondered how much of her impassioned speech was more for her sake than theirs.

Sean grinned at her. "Sounds to me like you're trying to talk yourself into the idea."

Lauren sighed. "Maybe I am. I'll admit I'm a little worried about pulling it off."

Sean lifted one of her feet and kissed the sole lightly. "You'll do fine, Ms. Four-Point-Oh. You always do."

"I appreciate your confidence. Now I just have to

figure out why someone would choose to give another person so much power over them. To be quite honest, I can't relate to the idea. Not even a little."

"When you say submissiveness, do you mean in a general sense or a sexual sense?" Sean asked, as a naughty idea invaded his mind.

"It's a Human Sexuality course," Lauren said, as if that should explain it all. "I'm looking at it from a bedroom perspective, of course."

"So what you're really researching is the idea of a Dom/sub relationship. I mean, you can't focus on one without understanding the other, right?"

Lauren considered his words then nodded. "I guess you're right. I hadn't thought that far yet."

"You know, I think I may have spoken too soon. I'd be more than happy to help you with this project."

Sean heard Chad's chuckle and muttered "I bet you would" from across the room. He glanced over and for a moment, Sean was struck by the look on Chad's face—a look that let him know his friend wouldn't mind helping Lauren do her homework either.

Lauren heard Chad's comment too but she didn't acknowledge it. "Very funny, Sean. I was kidding about the leather and whip thing."

Sean had caught glimpses through the years of Keira's relationship with her husband, Will. Though nothing was ever said, or even overtly seen, Sean suspected their sexual relationship was built on the sort of premise Lauren now had to explore. The same idea that had Sean's cock twitching in his jeans.

He tried to let the subject go, knew he should let it drop, but thinking before he spoke had never been his strong suit. "If you have to get into the mindset, wouldn't it be easier if you were experiencing some of the feelings, rather than just reading about them?"

Lauren sat up, her face portraying interest. "Are you saying I should pretend to submit to you in the bedroom?"

Sean shook his head. "I don't think you can pretend, Lauren. If you're serious about getting into the mind of a submissive, you would have to genuinely submit."

She frowned. "To you?"

Sean wished he could understand the mixture of emotions filling her green eyes. "Why not? It's not like we're not sexually active."

"You would want to do that?" she asked.

He nodded and just barely kept himself from saying "fuck yeah." He didn't want to scare her off, but if she knew how badly he wanted to command her sexually, she'd freak out. He'd hidden most of his more extreme desires. Now that their relationship had crossed the boundary from new and exciting to comfortable and predictable, he'd found it harder, rather than easier, to bring up the subject of doing a little experimenting in the bedroom.

"There are years of trust between us, Lauren. You know I wouldn't hurt you." Sean was intensely aware of the fact Chad was in the room, listening to every word. What was his friend thinking?

Lauren swallowed. "I don't know if I can do what you're asking."

"What would be holding you back?" Sean didn't realize until he'd heard her topic how much he wanted to explore this aspect of his personality. Maybe this would be the trick to putting a spark back into their relationship. They'd only had sex once since her kiss with Chad on Sunday, and it had felt...off.

"You really can't think of a few thousand things that might be holding me back?" Lauren put her hands up, waving them as if looking for the words. It was a habit of hers, talking with her hands, moving them a mile a minute. Sean and Chad had threatened to tie her hands several times just to see if she could talk without them.

Suddenly the image of Lauren standing between him and Chad, her hands bound behind her, sent his cock into red alert.

"I don't know. Let's see if I can list them for you. Number one, I don't take orders well. I never have. It wouldn't be easy to just hand myself over to you in the bedroom and say 'have at it'. Isn't this Dom/sub stuff all about whips and cuffs and shit like that? I'm not a fan of pain, you know. I cry over paper cuts."

Chad laughed, entering the conversation. "Jesus, Lauren. I hardly think that's how a Dom/sub relationship works. It's more about an exchange of power. I mean, being submissive doesn't mean being helpless."

Sean leaned forward. "Chad's right. It's built on compatible needs and desires, and trust plays a major role."

"But you'd also be letting someone test your limits. That's part of it too. You'd be allowing someone to push you further than you ever thought you could go," Chad added.

"What if I'm pushed too far?" Lauren asked.

Sean grasped her hand. "That's where the trust comes in."

Chad was leaning forward in his chair and Sean could sense his friend's genuine interest. "Think of it, Lauren. Imagine giving up control and letting someone test your limits, letting someone push you into an entirely different realm. Bondage, pain, sensory deprivation, sex in public, a ménage." The last word was spoken more softly than the others, but it seemed to resonate louder than a cannon shot.

The room fell silent, the air charged with something Sean couldn't define. Though the conversation had been hypothetical, it felt like something much more and there was no denying Chad wanted to master Lauren as badly as he did.

Lauren broke the uneasy silence, her voice tense despite her efforts to appear nonchalant. "Jeez. How many nights have the three of us sat together getting swept away in conversations like this? I have to say this one might take the cake."

Sean shrugged. "Curse of living with two psych majors. All you two ever want to do is talk, talk, talk." Psychology majors tended to confront things a bit too head-on for him sometimes, but the idea of acting on this particular conversation settled in his thoughts and wouldn't let go.

Ménage.

What if they stopped talking and started doing?

They were skirting around the issue, saying too much while saying nothing at all. It seemed to be a talent they'd all perfected over the years.

Chad, clearly uncomfortable, rose. "I'm heading out, doing a late dinner with Lily tonight. It was her birthday last Friday, but I didn't get to celebrate with her because Justin and K took her away for a romantic weekend."

Sean smiled. "Talked to Justin Monday. Sounds like they had a good time."

Chad gave a fake shiver. "Guess I'll have to listen to all the gory, sickly sweet details tonight. You guys want to come with me?"

Sean shook his head. "Hockey's on tonight."

"I'm going to start outlining some ideas for my project," Lauren said.

"Sounds like I'm on my own. I'll see you all later."

They listened as Chad grabbed a coat and his car keys, the front door closing behind him.

Lauren handed Sean the remote. "I'll take my laptop up to my room and work there."

Sean gave her a guilty grin. "I'll keep the volume down if you wanna work in here."

Lauren laughed. "You couldn't watch a hockey game without yelling obscenities if someone was holding a gun to your head. I'll come down in a little while and throw in a frozen pizza or something."

"Sounds good." Sean watched her head upstairs and he leaned back, not bothering to turn on the TV.

He closed his eyes, picturing Lauren sitting on her bed, her laptop open as she looked at pictures of women submitting to their men. He imagined her on her knees before him, taking his cock into her sweet mouth as he directed her movements, his fingers gripping her hair tightly. Then suddenly Chad was there. Lauren moved between them as she took turns sucking each, first his cock and then Chad's.

He wasn't sure how long he let the fantasy wrap itself around him, but it was full night outside when he pulled himself to the surface. He shifted uncomfortably on the couch, his cock pulsating against the constraining denim of his jeans. He was tempted to free the rock-hard flesh and administer a bit of relief with his own hand.

The idea of dominating Lauren in the bedroom was simply too powerful an aphrodisiac to resist. He'd always felt a vein of strength at his core. Always fought to restrain this uber-masculinity that society didn't seem to embrace anymore. His sisters jokingly called him and his brothers cavemen, but he couldn't fail to notice they'd all married men just like the Collins males. Take-charge men who would give anything, do anything, to protect their wives. It was an old-fashioned notion and though Sean fought to hide it, it didn't mean it wasn't there.

Fuck. For years he'd let Lauren call the shots in their relationship, let her determine their limits because he'd always known what he'd want from her and suspected his desires would scare her.

Now she needed to learn about submission and his restraint was in tatters. Maybe he could restate the offer to master her. He could tie it up in an "in the interest of research" bow to make her feel safe. He wanted Lauren, wanted her for the long haul, and was terrified of losing her. That kiss with Chad had changed something. He could see it. He just couldn't figure out how to fix it.

He rose slowly and paced around the living room a few times in an attempt to ease his erection. He couldn't go up to their bedroom like this. Once he'd gotten his arousal under control, he'd go upstairs and talk to her.

The only thing he couldn't figure out was where Chad fit into the equation, and that was the true setback to his problem. Because Sean knew for certain his friend was a big part of the solution.

Shit.

CHAPTER FOUR

L auren sighed and forced herself to work on her assignment, dragging her laptop to her bed. She was grateful for the distraction. This past week she'd been living in a self-imposed hell, trying to pretend she wasn't in love with two men. Chad's kiss had changed the question mark behind her feelings to a definite exclamation point. She was a goner.

Foolishly, she'd believed confessing about the kiss would make things easier, better, but it hadn't. Try as she may, she couldn't force her life to return to normal. She couldn't be with Sean without wishing Chad was there too and she couldn't hang out with Chad without wondering what Sean was thinking, remembering his desire to watch her kiss his best friend.

Stop it, Lauren. Do your damn homework.

She began typing key phrases into a search engine and before long she'd found a BDSM site with pictures. After studying several submissive poses, she clicked through a few links until she found the diary of a woman who lived as a sex slave. She was captivated by the woman's descriptions of her lifestyle, by her feelings, her needs.

Lauren closed her eyes after an hour of reading, putting herself in the woman's place. Only in her mind, Lauren didn't see one Dom, she saw two. Chad and Sean were standing before her as she knelt, naked. Her hands were tied behind her back and they were taking turns thrusting their hard cocks into her mouth, demanding she suck them, take them all the way.

She gasped at their strength, at the power of the moment. She was close, so close to coming, and she could tell they were too. Her fingers drifted inside her pants and she stroked her clit, gently at first, then harder and faster.

Just a few more rubs and—

Her cell phone rang.

Fuck.

Glancing at the caller ID, she suppressed a groan before answering.

"Hi, Riley." Her voice came out more breathless than she'd intended.

"Hey, chickie, what's shakin'?"

"Nothing." Lauren cleared her throat. "Just doing some research."

"Research? It sounds like you've been running on the treadmill. What kind of research?"

Lauren closed her eyes and prayed for patience. "What do you mean what kind? Just research."

"Your voice sounds funny."

Lauren feigned a cough. "I think I'm getting a cold."

Riley laughed. "Liar, liar, pants on fire. You were having sex, weren't you?"

"No. Absolutely not. I'm sitting here by myself."

"Fine. Then you were masturbating," she deadpanned.

"There's no way you can tell that from my voice."

"Dildo or hand?"

Lauren shook her head. "You are a perverted woman."

Riley wasn't swayed. "Must be watching porn. Video or internet?"

"I'm not having this conversation," she said. Then Lauren heard a male voice in the background. "Is Aaron there? Jeez. Is he listening?"

"Yep. He told me to leave you alone."

Lauren smiled. Aaron rocked. "Tell him thanks for me."

"You know you don't have to play alone. You've got a boyfriend and a spare living in that house. Seduce one or, better yet, both of them."

Lauren reclined on her bed, Riley's words reminding her of her earlier conversation with Sean and Chad. For a moment, as the three of them talked about her assignment, she got the sense both men would be more than willing to help with her homework.

"You're right. I should."

She heard Riley's quick intake of breath. "I'm right? You're finally admitting you want a threesome?"

"I never said I *didn't* want it. I just said a threesome

would be too complicated. I still stand by that belief. The thing is…" She paused, uncertain if she should tell Riley exactly where her desires were leading her now.

"The thing is what?" Riley prodded.

"I have a new assignment in my Human Sexuality class."

Lauren could just picture Riley's excitement. "What kind of assignment? Something kinky?"

"Sort of. I have to put myself in the mindset of a submissive."

Riley whistled. "You need to talk to Keira."

Lauren was stunned by Riley's response. "Keira? Why?"

"Because I'm pretty sure she and Will live in a sort of Dom/sub lifestyle."

Lauren shook her head. "No way. Your sister is the most self-sufficient, confident, take-charge woman I know. There's no way she lets Will push her around in the bedroom."

"Push her around? Oh man, Lauren. You really *do* need to talk to Keira. I think you may have some misguided ideas about BDSM."

Lauren took Riley's words as an insult. "Oh right, and I suppose you're a pro at the whole submitting-to-your-man thing. I'd love to see Aaron try to—"

"Aaron totally takes charge in the bedroom—and I fucking love it."

Riley's admission sent Lauren's entire world hurling off-kilter. "What?"

"Little bondage, some spanking, a few of his deep-voiced commands and he can set me off like a rocket."

Lauren tried to imagine Riley giving anyone the upper hand. *"Really?"*

Riley laughed. "Really. Listen. You're coming to Natalie's baby shower tomorrow night, right?"

Lauren nodded then remembered she was on the phone. Her mind was whirling with all this new information about the Collins women. "Yes, I'm coming."

"Keira will be here. You can talk to her about your assignment and then you and I are making a game plan."

"Game plan?" Lauren asked.

"Yep. You're gonna use this assignment to get everything you want and maybe even some stuff you didn't know you wanted."

"Like what?"

Lauren could picture Riley rubbing her hands together as she plotted. "You're going to get a lesson in submissiveness from *two* masters."

"Sean *and* Chad?"

Riley giggled. "Oh hell yeah. I have a feeling they'll both jump at the chance. Then once you have them both in your bedroom, you just have to make sure they stay there."

"This is never gonna work."

"Oh ye of little faith. We'll work out the details tomorrow at the shower. And Lauren?"

"Yeah?"

"Bet you get an A-plus on this assignment."

Riley hung up and left Lauren struggling to figure out

what can of worms she'd just opened. She'd inadvertently given Riley a mission. A dangerous proposition in the best of situations.

Worst of all, Lauren had a feeling she was going to go along with everything Riley said—because she really wanted to. She closed her eyes. Imagined Chad and Sean undressing her, touching her, kissing her—

"How's the research coming along?"

Lauren opened her eyes, quickly minimizing the browser before setting her laptop on the nightstand and looking up. Sean stood in the doorframe, smiling at her. She wondered what he saw when he looked at her. She didn't need a mirror to know her face was flushed. Shit, she'd been close to slipping her hands into her lounge pants again and bringing about the orgasm building inside her.

"Fine," she said, the word sticking in her throat. She cleared it but remained quiet, unable to say more, afraid she'd give herself away.

Sean's gaze narrowed and she fought to clear her face of expression. Sean was too savvy, too smart. "Find anything interesting?"

She shook her head. She couldn't have this conversation with him. Hell, she couldn't have *any* conversation with him right now. She was too hot, too bothered, too fucking close to coming. "Not yet. I think I changed my mind about pizza. I'm going to keep working up here for a little while." She'd promised Sean she'd never cheat on him, but if he touched her now there was no way she could lay with him and not think about Chad. Her gaze drifted to her nightstand drawer. The second he left, she was locking herself in, surrendering to her ménage fantasy and taking care of business with her vibrator.

Then she needed to figure out what the fuck she was going to do next. She was screwing up every relationship in her life that mattered to her.

Sean walked into the room, closing the door behind him and not stopping until he'd reached the bed. "I've been thinking." He sank down beside her on the mattress.

Screw the vibrator. The moment Sean leaned closer, her body went into overdrive. Being close to him never failed to provoke a red-hot need.

"Oh yeah?" She forced an easygoing tone to her voice. "Thinking about what?"

"Your dilemma."

She frowned. "I don't have a dilemma."

"You need to learn about submission."

She waved at the computer screen. "I'm finding plenty of stuff. I don't think this will be as hard as I thought."

"I thought you weren't supposed to Google for information. I thought you needed to take a more up-close and personal look at it." He leaned forward as he spoke. She could smell the sweet scent of soda on his breath.

She loved Sean, loved being physically close to him, but most of all, she loved his kisses. He sure as hell knew his way around her mouth. It had been over two years since their first kiss, but every time his lips met hers was just as exciting and new as that original kiss.

"Up-close and personal?"

"Haven't you even wondered, Lauren?"

Her eyebrows creased at his question. "About what?"

"Us. What it would be like to expand on our bedroom experiences. Our sex is still hot...fucking knocks my socks off, but wouldn't you like to see if we could go higher, find more?"

"I suppose I've thought about it." What would he say if she told him exactly how far her secret desires had wandered?

"I've given it a lot of thought," he confessed. "And I've decided I'm sick of wondering."

She knew what he wanted. She also knew it was time to stop lying. To him and to herself. When she submitted her body, her mind and her soul, she wanted it to be with him *and* Chad. Her heart was split down the middle and it wasn't fair to Sean to only offer him half. "Sean, I can't—"

"Just hear me out, Lauren. I'm offering a compromise."

"Another one?" she joked. Her mind drifted to the foosball table that still sat in the dining room.

He grinned. "I want to dominate you and you want an A. Let's work on your project together."

"You honestly think I'd agree to submit to you just to get a good grade in a class? Jesus, either I'm a huge nerd or a callous bitch or both, but either way, I hardly think—"

Sean shook his head. "That came out wrong. I saw your face when I walked in here. The research is getting to you, isn't it? I saw the flush on your cheeks. I can tell when a woman is on the verge of an orgasm. You like what you're reading. You want to try it."

"Some dreams are best left alone."

His gaze sharpened. "So you're admitting it's a dream of yours?"

She wanted to bite off her foolish tongue. "I didn't expect to— I didn't realize how affected I would be..." She paused and tried to find a way to say what she was thinking. She did want to submit, but not to just Sean.

"You didn't know the idea of submission would turn you on so much, make you so hot you could melt. If I reached into your panties, how wet would I find you?"

"Drenched," she whispered before closing her eyes. "Shit. That's not important."

"I'd say that's pretty fucking important."

One look at his face proved he was finished asking. She'd never seen him look more determined...or hungry.

"Lauren, we've been together for years. I love you. I respect your intelligence and your independence—but right now, I want to possess you, show you how much more I have to offer."

His words struck a chord. She'd been trying to play by the rules for years, becoming increasingly more miserable as each day passed. She'd been so intent on maintaining a normal relationship that she'd failed to realize how much she was missing, how much she was hurting. She owed it to Sean to tell him the truth. To tell him how she felt about Chad...but she was too afraid. Even as she sat here, she knew they were talking about two different things. He wanted to explore BDSM. She wanted Chad.

"When did life get so complicated?"

He grinned. "There's nothing complicated about this. You just have to give yourself to me, Lauren. Submit to me."

He backed his words up with a kiss and she let herself be swept away. For several moments, she simply let her lips say all the things she couldn't find the words to express. She *did* want him. She *did* want this. Problem was...she wanted so much more.

The tenor of the touches changed. Sean's lips firmed and he pressed harder. His tongue no longer seemed to stroke her mouth as much as it came in and conquered. Always a gentle lover, Sean took her by surprise with his rough kiss.

He pushed her down on the bed, coming over her, never breaking the union of their lips. He reached up with his hands, tangling them in her ponytail, tugging at her hair. Her body flew into overdrive with his forceful grasp. She spread her legs and wrapped them around his hips as he began to drive his jeans-covered cock against her pussy. Desperation seemed to lace Sean's movement. Lauren wondered what prompted it.

He continued to lay siege to her lips and though she tried to break away, tried to put some distance between them in an effort to find air, he held her immobile, hostage to his whims.

"Sean," she whispered, but he swallowed her words, kissing her harder, driving his tongue into her mouth.

Her mind fought him, tried to force this stranger away, but her body was held in his thrall. She tightened her legs as he thrust against her faster. He was driving her arousal higher with each touch, each unspoken demand.

She tried one last-ditch attempt at feeble resistance. Dragging her nails along his back, she scratched him. Hard. She grinned when she heard his hiss of pain. She'd scored a point.

She was surprised when he released her hair and reached for her hands. Grasping them tightly by the wrists, he pulled them above her head, holding them against the mattress.

"Trust me," he said against her lips, his words deep, powerful. He didn't give her a chance to respond. He merely punctuated his command with another hard kiss.

She tried once more to free her lips from his. She needed to breathe, needed space between them so she could think. He was driving her arousal higher with each touch until she found it impossible to form a coherent thought. He adjusted his grip, holding both her hands with one of his while the other took control of her head. His implacable clasp told her he could easily possess her.

She continued to fight, to struggle—though the effort was halfhearted at best. The combined feeling of his cock against her needy center, his fingers in her hair, his lips and mouth consuming her as he held her immobile against the bed, was working some sort of magic on her.

His tongue swept along her lower lip before diving into her mouth again. Suddenly the fight went out of her. She brushed her tongue against his, letting her arms lay slack in his grip.

She understood. She knew now where it was Sean wanted to take her and for the briefest of moments, submitting to him sounded heavenly. She was tired of fighting him, fighting her attraction to Chad, fighting this incredible feeling. To hell with the consequences. She knew wherever Sean led, she'd follow willingly.

The hand holding her ponytail loosened and Sean pulled away only an inch, his gaze capturing hers.

He gave her a victorious grin. "You're mine, Lauren."

She tried to assimilate his words while the riotous emotions rocketed through her body. One word kept pounding in her brain, taking up the same rhythm as the blood coursing through her veins.

Submit. Submit. Submit.

Isn't that what she'd just done? Put herself in Sean's hands? Given him control of her body? Yes. She had. She thought she'd be more uncomfortable with the realization, but her mind and body seemed to agree on only one thing. She wanted to give him everything she had to offer, but she needed more.

Sean pulled her T-shirt over her head, bending down to take her pebbled nipple between his lips. He sucked hard, the rough suction sending impulses along every part of her body. She pushed her hips against his, needing more stimulation, more sensation. Her body was on fire, held hostage by his mastery.

As he stripped her pants off, she reached to shed his clothing as well.

"Put your hands back on the bed." His voice was deep, firm.

"I want to see you."

Sean paused. That charged moment was all she needed. His face told her he would have his way on this and she put her hands back on the pillow by her head.

"I know what you need, Lauren," he said. "Now let me give it to you."

His lips returned to hers and his kiss washed away every other thought. All she needed was relief.

Then, the image of Chad's face flashed in her mind.

"God," she groaned when he pulled away to suck on her breast once more. Her mind was running in a million different directions, her emotions on system overload. Sean moved farther away, knelt between her open legs. His gaze drifted from her pussy, slowly up her body until it landed on her face.

Then he reached forward and pressed a finger inside her. She groaned. She'd been waiting for that touch but it still wasn't enough.

"You need more," he said, his eyes holding hers captive.

She nodded.

"Tell me what," he prompted.

"Another finger," she whispered.

He complied, adding a second finger to the first, the

thrusts still shallow, still not creating the incredible friction she'd grown accustomed to.

"You need more," he repeated. "Tell me."

"Harder," she begged. "Faster."

Again he took her at his words, driving her to the peak of her climax quickly. Even as her body flushed with heat and need, it wasn't enough.

"Tell me," he said once more. "I'll give you everything you need, Lauren. Everything."

"You." She reached for him but he was too far away. His eyes narrowed and she remembered she wasn't supposed to move. She put her hands back on the bed. Pleased by her acquiescence, he quickly opened his pants, bent forward, placed his cock at the entrance to her body and shoved inside in one firm, hard, beautiful thrust. He filled her in an instant, a millisecond, but still...

"What else, Lauren?"

Her eyes had closed when he'd entered her, but now they flew open. "What?"

He smiled, setting a steady rhythm as he fucked her into oblivion. Even as he moved, she knew he waited for an answer.

Her body was flying on autopilot, heading toward the orgasm it desired, and basically it didn't give a shit about the fact he wanted to talk.

"God," she cried, when he hit that one spot, deep inside. Lights flashed behind her eyelids. She reached up, gripped the tops of his strong arms, searching for something to anchor her to this spot, this moment.

"Tell me." Sean paused just seconds before her climax. Her body trembled in pain as he withheld what she needed most.

"No!" she yelled, but he didn't move.

"You want more, Lauren. All you have to do is ask."

She found it difficult to breathe, the air in the room stifling hot.

As she looked into his beloved face, she saw determined lines around his eyes and mouth and in that instant, she realized.

He knew what was missing.

"Chad," she whispered.

He smiled and began to thrust harder, faster. Somehow she'd freed them both with her confession. It was out in the open. With her confession made, she felt lighter, freer, alive. Her hips rose to meet Sean's, the pounding pleasure of his lovemaking driving her straight into the white-hot magic.

She screamed as she came, a cacophony of words flying from her lips, Sean's name, Chad's name, words of love and forever.

"Yes," she heard Sean hiss, and then she felt the hot splashes of his release fill her.

He would give her everything she wanted. Everything.

For several moments they clung to each other and Lauren let herself remain adrift in the blissful aftermath. The real world would return too soon.

"You're in love with him." Sean didn't seem surprised or even sad, his words a statement rather than a question.

He rolled away, claiming his side of the bed as he faced her.

With some distance between them, her head felt clearer and her senses returned.

"Yes," she admitted. "I love you, Sean. I really do. It's just—"

"You love him too."

She smiled sadly. "I love him too. Do you hate me?"

Sean chuckled. "God no. Never."

She fell silent. His words so typically, wonderfully Sean.

"We have time, Lauren. I meant what I said. I'll give you everything you want. You just have to trust me. For now, sleep."

She curled against his shoulder as he engulfed her in his large embrace. For once, she wasn't trying to solve the puzzle. For once, she gave up all her internal struggles and placed herself in Sean's capable, strong hands. And for the first time in a long time, she felt happy.

CHAD'S LEGS gave out and he let the wall support him as he slid slowly to the floor, his mind trying to process what he'd just heard.

He'd returned from dinner with Lily, exhausted, nothing on his mind except falling into bed. As he reached the top of the stairs, he'd heard the creaking mattress. He'd been tempted to turn around and go back to the living room to sleep on the couch.

Then Lauren had screamed.

Sean's name—and his.

His.

Stunned, he stared at the closed door to Lauren and Sean's bedroom, trying to figure out what the hell that meant. Sean must have heard her. Yet the door remained closed. The room quiet.

And Chad stayed on the floor, staring at the door, wishing he were on the other side.

CHAPTER FIVE

Lauren looked around the room full of women and grinned. She took another sip of Riley's famous vodka punch, perfectly aware of the fact she'd already consumed too much of the stuff. She didn't care though. Chances were she'd have lots more before the night was over. The alcohol was dulling the sharp pain that had been slicing through her heart since waking this morning to find Sean gone. Granted, he'd had to work, but the distance had given her too much time to think, to doubt. Chad had been suspiciously absent as well and she was now a bundle of nerves as she questioned everything that had happened last night.

She'd escaped her silent torture a few hours earlier, volunteering to help Riley decorate for the shower in an attempt to think of anything other than how she was royally fucking up her life.

More laughter pulled Lauren from her heavy thoughts

and she pushed them away, determined to enjoy the evening. Riley and her friend Bubbles had organized what was quite possibly the craziest baby shower she'd ever attended.

They'd just finished played Pin the Diaper on the Bad Baby. She wasn't sure where Riley had found all the posters of hot, naked men, but Lauren was hoping Riley would let her take the cowboy one home. Prior to that, Lauren had kicked ass in the baby bottle chugging contest, though Lily had given her a run for her money. The ladies in attendance had already consumed one large bowl of the punch and were currently working their way through the second batch.

Natalie, the mother-to-be and one of the few remaining sober women in the room, was almost finished opening the pile of shower gifts and was currently wiping away a happy tear as Teagan strummed the last chord in the lullaby she'd written for Nat's baby.

Lauren had gotten to know most of the Collins women quite well over the years through her relationship with Sean. They'd never failed to make her feel like one of their own. She watched Natalie gently rub the large bulge of her belly and she knew Ewan and Nat's baby was one of the luckiest kids in the world. She could only imagine how awesome it would be to grow up with such a large and loving family.

A tap on her shoulder pulled Lauren from her thoughts and she turned to see Keira standing behind her. "Riley said you wanted to talk to me."

Lauren nodded, suddenly feeling nervous. The cowardly part of her had actually decided tonight wasn't a good night to approach Keira. A quick glance at Riley's smug smile told her that her friend knew she'd planned to chicken out.

"I, um..." She cleared her throat. "I have an assignment for class, but now might not be a good time. I mean, it's your sister-in-law's baby shower and I'm not sure—"

Keira raised a hand to cut her off. "Now is fine. The presents are almost all opened and I have a feeling Riley has another twisted game planned. If I drink too much more of that punch tonight, I'll be dancing on the tables soon. Of course, Will likes it when I dance for him."

Lauren laughed. "Actually, it was sort of you and Will I wanted to talk about." Lauren lifted her glass and tossed back the rest of her spiked punch, hoping it would relax her. How was she supposed to ask Keira about her submissive lifestyle?

Although, after discovering the buttons Sean had pushed in her last night, it was clear she needed to get some answers to her questions. She was on the verge of spontaneously combusting from the bonfire of lust this assignment had fueled in her body. She needed to know what this meant. If it was normal.

Keira smiled kindly. "Come on. Let's top up these drinks and find somewhere quiet." Keira refilled both their glasses and they headed down the hallway to the kitchen as the rest of the party broke into howls of laughter. Bubbles was explaining the rules to the next game, something involving banana baby food and pacifiers.

As they entered the kitchen, Keira took a seat at the table, gesturing to the chair next to her. "I swear to God only *my* sister would ask an ex-Vegas hooker to organize games for a baby shower."

Lauren sank down in the seat. "Yeah, I know. Bubbles is great. I'm having a blast."

"Me too. Riley told me what your assignment was about."

Lauren tried to decide if she was annoyed with or grateful to her friend. "She did?"

Keira nodded. "You have to explore the submissive lifestyle for a paper in your Human Sexuality class."

Lauren toyed with her glass. "And you don't think it's odd Riley wanted me to talk to *you* about that particular subject?"

Keira's soft laughter immediately set Lauren's mind at ease. She'd always admired Sean's oldest sister. She was one of the few people Lauren had ever met who genuinely fit in her own skin. "Is that your subtle way of asking me if Riley's right? If I'm submissive?"

Lauren gave her a guilty grin. "I hate to pry."

"You aren't prying. I initiated the conversation, remember? If I didn't want to talk about it, I would have told Riley to forget it and we'd be out there playing that perverted pacifier game."

"How do you know it's perverted?" Lauren asked,

looking over her shoulder as another round of cheers and laughter rose in the living room.

Keira feigned a shudder. "Bubbles called it the 'Banana Suckers' game. Do I really need to say more?"

They laughed and Lauren relaxed. She felt her concerns easing. "I don't get it."

"Get what?" Keira asked.

"You're one of the most self-sufficient, strong women I've ever met. I guess I don't understand why you would give all that up in the bedroom."

Keira rested her chin on her hand and sighed. "Have you done any research on this subject yet?" Lauren nodded, confused by the question until Keira clarified, "And in that research, does it say that the submissive gives up all control?"

Lauren considered her question. In one article, the submissive woman commented on feeling more powerful than her Dom, but the words seemed in direct contradiction to the scene the woman was describing. "Not exactly, but—"

"Not at all. Lauren, I'm the oldest of seven kids. My mom died when I was in high school and I spent nearly a decade trying to be what I thought my family needed. You see me as strong and self-sufficient and that makes me happy. It's a wonderful compliment you've paid me, but I didn't become any of those things until I gave my heart, my soul and my body over to Will."

Lauren sighed. "Again with the contradictions. That doesn't make sense."

Keira took a sip of her punch and winced slightly. "I think Riley made this second batch stronger than the first. Maybe it does sound like a contradiction, but consider this. When I met Will, I was burning the candle at both ends—working full-time in the pub, attending college, trying to be a mother to my brothers and sisters. I'm afraid Sean caught the brunt of my smothering since he was the youngest. I was a bundle of pent-up nerves and anxieties, encased in an exhausted body. In a word, I was a mess."

"And Will changed that?"

Keira smiled. "Will changed everything. I swear sometimes it feels like I'm this solid form to everyone else, but to him, I'm transparent. He saw all the jumbled-up craziness inside me and he introduced me to his lifestyle."

Lauren blushed as she imagined Keira's handsome husband in leather, wielding a whip.

Keira must've understood her look perfectly, because she laughed. "There's more to the lifestyle than silly accoutrements."

Lauren shook her head. "I'm sorry. I'm not usually so naïve and juvenile. I think I'm a bit tired tonight. I've had too much of this damn punch. Feels like my brain is slogging through mud."

Keira leaned back and studied her face. Lauren knew the pose well. It was one she'd employed numerous times in her psychology classes. Unfortunately, she was used to being the studier, not the studied. "You're overwrought."

Lauren frowned. "No, I'm not. I'm fine."

"You remind me a lot of myself, Lauren."

Lauren shook her head. "Thank you, Keira, but no. While you've fought to overcome some difficult things—losing your mom to cancer, taking care of your pop and your family—my life's been a piece of cake. I mean, my folks are happily married and helping me achieve my college degree, my brother and I have a pretty cool relationship, though I don't see him as much as I'd like. I'm only working part-time, which certainly isn't wearing me out. I'm just nice, normal, boring Lauren."

"And nice, normal, boring Lauren is in love with two men."

Lauren's face flushed hotly. "Riley told you?" Her tone betrayed her anger and hurt.

Keira shook her head. "No. She didn't."

"Then who?"

"Actually, it was Will who pointed it out once. My hubby is too observant."

Lauren closed her eyes. "Great. Like that's not completely embarrassing."

Keira reached across the table to take Lauren's hand. "Oh no. I didn't say that to embarrass you. Will just observed that there were some unexplored feelings between the three of you. Honestly, until he said it, I'd had no idea. Then I started looking more closely."

"Yeah, well. I'm not sure how unexplored they are." She wasn't sure why she was confessing so much to Keira, but something about the woman told Lauren her trust wouldn't be misplaced.

"Meaning?"

"Meaning Sean's sort of offered to help me research this particular topic."

Keira grinned. "The ménage or the submission?"

"Both."

Her answer caused Keira to giggle. "I bet he did. I've always suspected there was a bit of a closeted Dom in my baby brother. I have a feeling your assignment is a bit like waving a red flag in front of a bull. Chances are good you aren't the only person who's going to learn something from this assignment."

"It's not Sean who needs to be convinced."

Keira frowned. "Chad's not interested?"

Lauren shrugged. "I have no idea where Chad's interests lie." The words weren't exactly the truth. The kiss they'd shared told her Chad wanted her, and his face as they had discussed submission definitely betrayed his desire to play the Dom.

"Ah," Keira said, as Lauren watched understanding dawn in the other woman's face. "So your problem is actually twofold."

"Meaning?" Lauren asked.

"You want to explore submission, but you also want to engage in a ménage with Chad and Sean."

Lauren put her head on her arms on top of the table. "This is impossible. I'm not the kind of girl who can do one of those things, let alone both."

"Why not?"

Lauren raised her head slightly. "I told you why.

Remember me? Boring, normal Lauren? You're the brave one."

"Comparing yourself to me isn't fair. Saying that your life has been all sunshine and roses, so you can't follow my path, is just wrong. You know that."

"Yeah. I know that. You wouldn't know I'm the psych major in this conversation, would you? You missed your calling, Keira. And I'm obviously in the wrong field."

"It's easy to recognize and categorize other people's problems because there are no emotions attached to them."

Lauren sat up and nodded. "I think it's safe to say I have every emotion under the sun rolling around in me right now—love, lust, confusion, loneliness, depression, happiness..." She paused then added, "Vodka," with a laugh.

"I was dealing with all of those same feelings when I started dating Will and I was exhausted. He taught me to let go of the reins, showed me it was okay to shrug off the heavy load every now and again and let someone else carry it. I make a hundred decisions during the day at work. I worry constantly about my family. Pop's health, Natalie's pregnancy, Teagan and Sky on the road all the time, Sean. When I go home at night, Will's there, waiting for me. He's shown me how to clear my mind, how to trust and love and feel. Believe me, after a night in his arms, I wake up every morning refreshed and ready to take on the world again."

Lauren nodded, Keira's words making sense after her experience with Sean the previous night. For a little while, she'd put herself completely into his hands and it had felt more wonderful that she could have imagined.

Riley came into the kitchen before Lauren could reply. "Hey, are you two finished? We're about to start making a list of all the names Natalie can scream at Ewan while she's in labor. We're thinking she needs something stronger than 'asswipe' and 'fucking bastard'."

Keira laughed. "That sounds like fun. God knows I flung a few colorful expletives at Will when I was having Caitlyn and PJ." She looked at Lauren. "You can call me any time, you know. If you have more questions."

"I might take you up on that." They both rose. "Thanks, Keira. For everything."

"Things will work out the way they're supposed to, Lauren. You just have to hang in there until they do."

Lauren nodded and started to follow Keira to the living room, but Riley stopped her. "That's bullshit."

"What's bullshit?" Lauren asked.

"Keira's 'hang in there' comment. You can't just sit around and wait for life to happen to you, Lauren."

"I don't think that's what I'm doing."

Riley rolled her eyes. "That's *all* you're doing. So here's the plan." She tugged Lauren back to the table and they sat down. "When you go home tonight, you tell those clueless fuckers you live with—"

"You know, one of those clueless fuckers is your brother," Lauren interrupted.

"So who would know better than me that he's clueless and blind and an idiot?"

Lauren laughed. "Man, you take sisterly love to a whole new level, don't you?"

Riley narrowed her eyes. "Are you finished stalling? Do you want to hear my plan?"

What Lauren wanted to do was kick her own ass for even thinking of taking Riley's advice. What she said was, "Lay it on me."

SEAN WALKED into the office where Chad was working and plopped onto the chair where Lauren usually sat.

"Something wrong?" Chad asked, without looking away from his computer screen. Sean had been uncharacteristically quiet since returning home from the pub over an hour ago. Chad had worried all day about Sean's response to Lauren calling out his name during their lovemaking. He'd sort of expected Sean to beat the shit out of him and kick him out of the house the second he returned from work. Now, given Sean's silence, he didn't know what to expect.

"Lauren's in love with you."

Chad looked up, his lips instantly numb with shock. "What?"

Sean shrugged casually, but the nonchalant act wasn't fooling Chad. "I went upstairs after you left. Told her I was serious about helping her explore submissiveness."

"And?" Chad forced himself to breathe slowly and easily.

"And one thing led to another and she told me she's in love with both of us."

Chad closed his eyes and tried to make his brain function. Lauren had confessed to being in love with him? She *loved* him? Obviously Sean and Lauren had had quite the heart-to-heart last night. Part of him was glad he'd missed it, but that thought immediately left him feeling like a coward. He sucked at sharing his feelings, opting to let Sean and Lauren be the emotional weather vanes in the house. It was easier for him to assume a poker face, keep things buried.

"You must be mistaken."

Sean shook his head. "Nope. No mistake."

Sean's words took a few moments to penetrate. Even when they did, all he could say was, "I'm sorry."

Sean's gaze was piercing when it caught his. "Why?"

Chad frowned. "Because she's your girlfriend. Because the two of you bought this house with plans to get married and have a life together. What happens now?"

"I would think that's obvious."

Chad leaned forward in his chair and raked a hand through his hair. Sometimes talking to Sean was like holding a conversation with an alien from Mars. There was a definite language barrier. "There's an obvious answer to this?"

"Yep."

Chad rested his elbows on his knees and prayed for the patience to make it through this frustrating, shocking conversation. "And it is?"

Sean tilted his head to the side and grinned. "She gets both of us."

"Both of us. No. No, Sean. There's no way that would work."

"Of course it would. Hell, we're all living together. We're friends. We're attracted to her and she's attracted to us. I'd say this is a no-brainer. Sort of kicking myself for not suggesting it sooner."

Sean's words hit Chad in the chest like a bullet. "Are you insane?"

While Sean might not see the potential problem in what he was suggesting, Chad could see it clearer than a flashing neon sign.

Sean crossed his arms over his chest and leaned back in his chair. The posture immediately told Chad his friend was settling in for the long haul in hopes of convincing him to see his way of thinking. It was a pose Chad was very familiar with.

Let's streak at the football tailgate.

Let's sneak into the cheerleaders' locker room.

Let's ditch work to hit the strip club.

No matter what Sean suggested, when he assumed "the pose", Chad knew he was done for. Not this time.

"I'm not insane. I happen to think this is the first decision I've made in a long time that makes sense. Dammit, Chad. You and I both know this can work. We've seen a threesome up-close and personal for years in our own families. Lily, Justin and K are living proof that it can work."

Chad turned toward his computer, unable to face his

friend as he avoided the truth of Sean's words. "Lauren's my friend. I love her, but I'm not about to thrust her into a ménage relationship."

Sean was silent for several painfully long moments and then he asked the question Chad dreaded. "Why not?"

Chad's temper sparked. Why was Sean leading them down this road? "You know why the fuck not," he yelled. "Didn't we cover this territory in high school? You aren't *really* talking about a relationship like your brother and my sister share, are you?"

Sean ran his hand through his dark brown hair, the gesture a sure sign he was agitated, upset, and Chad tried to calm down. This conversation was hard enough without throwing anger into the mix.

Sean tugged his hair harder and Chad felt a twinge of guilt in his gut. He'd seen Sean use the same move time and time again throughout the years. Chad recalled worrying when they were just nine years old that Sean would pull all his hair out with during the months when Sean's mother, Sunday, was dying.

"We'd share Lauren," Sean murmured, looking at him. "Just Lauren. Nothing more. I swear."

Chad shook his head. "Please try to understand, Sean."

"I can't live without her."

Chad's lungs constricted as he saw the pain in his friend's face. Sean's feelings for Lauren ran even deeper than he'd realized—and he recognized his own were just as strong. He'd do anything for her happiness, for Sean's. "I'll walk away. Take myself out of the equation permanently."

Sean looked at him, studied his face far too closely. "You honestly expect me to sit here and ask you to cut out your own heart?" He shook his head. "No, Chad. That's not the answer."

"Then what is?"

Sean rose, exploding with the same frustration Chad was experiencing. "How the fuck do I know? As far as I can see, there's only one. We can't go on like we have been. That's not working for any of us."

Chad could see the sense in Sean's words and now that so much was out in the open, he found it impossible to hold back his true thoughts. "The past few years have sucked."

Sean sighed. "I know." His friend shrugged and smiled sadly. "Ball's in your court." Then he walked out of the room, leaving Chad alone with his confusing, agonizing thoughts.

Sean was right. There was one answer to their problem. Only one.

And it was the one Chad could never agree to.

CHAPTER SIX

A couple hours later, Chad looked up from his computer when he heard loud giggling in the yard. He was almost to the front door when Sean emerged from the kitchen.

"Is that Lauren?" Sean asked.

Chad shrugged. "Sounds like her."

He pulled the door open, surprised to find an intoxicated Lauren struggling to put her key in the lock as Aaron, dressed in his police uniform, stood next to her.

"Lauren? Are you drunk?" Chad asked.

Lauren giggled. "Just a little."

Aaron rolled his eyes and grinned. "I'm not here in an official capacity," Aaron said, when he spotted the concern in Chad's eyes.

Sean walked up behind him. "I thought you were at Natalie's baby shower?"

Lauren laughed again and stumbled slightly as she

crossed the threshold. "I was. It was fun." She walked into the house and toward the living room.

Chad turned to Aaron, who was shaking his head. "Apparently my wife throws a helluva baby shower," he said. "I got off-duty about an hour ago. I've been playing taxi driver since then. The mother-to-be was the only sober lady in the house when I got home. The rest of them were drunk as skunks. For some asinine reason, Riley put Bubbles in charge of the games. When I showed up, they were doing some beer chugging contest with baby bottles and from what I understand, it was a rematch between Lauren and Lily."

"My *sister* Lily?" Chad asked.

Sean laughed and said, "Sounds like we missed a great party."

Aaron shook his head. "Jesus, Sean. Only you would be sorry about missing a drunken baby shower. And no worries, Chad. I dropped Lily off just before heading here. I'm going home now. Lauren was my last delivery." He chuckled as he raised his hand to wave. "Night."

"Good night, Aaron," Chad said. "Thanks for bringing her home. I'll drive her by your place tomorrow to pick up her car."

Aaron nodded and walked to the curb where his car was parked.

Chad closed and locked the door. "So much for marriage settling Riley down."

Sean grinned. "Since my sisters have gotten married and started having kids, they don't get many crazy girl nights out. I'm glad Riley threw them a fun party, gave them a chance to let their hair down."

"Guess we should go check on *our* crazy girl." Chad stumbled briefly over the rightness of the word *our*. "Have to admit I can count on one hand the number of times I've seen her drunk."

Sean turned toward the living room. "I know. She never drinks. Wonder what got into her tonight."

"Probably Riley's influence."

Sean stopped and looked at him. "Maybe. I think Riley has been a good influence on Lauren these past few years. She's less stressed-out, less serious all the time. She was always sweet and nice, but Riley's softened some of the rougher edges, taught her to relax a bit."

Chad gave his friend a funny look and shook his head. "Riley didn't do that, Sean. You did."

"What?"

Chad was surprised Sean couldn't see it. "You've been the calming influence in Lauren's life. God knows I'm too much like her to make any significant change in her personality. She's loosened up, become more laid-back since dating you."

"You're crazy." Sean tried to cast off his compliment and Chad felt a wave of annoyance creep in.

"No, I'm not. You're a good influence on Lauren...on a lot of people." He added the last wondering if his best friend would understand that by "people" he meant himself. He'd been stewing over their earlier conversation, wallowing in guilt for hours. He was hurting Sean because of his own selfishness and fear. It was a treatment Sean sure as hell didn't deserve, given the unwavering friendship he'd offered Chad throughout the years.

The sound of something hitting the floor, followed by Lauren's loud "oops", distracted them. Sean laughed and the moment passed.

"Better go save our damsel in distress," Chad said. As they walked into the living room, they watched as Lauren picked up the magazines she'd knocked over.

"Bit clumsy tonight," she said as they came in.

"Can't imagine why." Sean bent over to help her put the magazines on the end table. "Have fun?"

"Ohmigod, yeah. Your sister knows how to throw one helluva shower."

Sean stood before helping Lauren rise.

Lauren rose up on tiptoe to place a kiss on Sean's lips. "Thanks," she said, wrapping her arms around Sean's neck and holding on.

"Um, Lauren?" Sean said, placing his hands on her hips when she started pushing herself against him.

"I've been thinking about your offer," she said.

Chad froze at her words. What offer was she referring to? Submission? A ménage? Did she even realize he was in the room?

"What offer is that?" Sean asked.

"I trust you," she said, as if her words answered his question.

"That's good. I trust you too," Sean replied.

"I trust both of you," she added, turning her head to

look at Chad. Yep, she knew he was there. He swallowed heavily at the sensuous look she was sending his way.

He wanted to respond. Fought for the right answer, but remained speechless.

"So I've decided," she continued. "I want you two to teach me how to submit."

If Chad hadn't been so shocked, he would have laughed at the image of Sean's jaw dropping open at her proclamation.

"Um, Lauren," Chad said. "Maybe tonight isn't the best time to discuss this. I mean, you've had a bit to drink and—"

"That's why this is the best time to talk about it. I want to say this tonight while my inhibitions are low. Then I want you two to think about my proposition. We can decide tomorrow when I'm sober."

Sean's gaze narrowed as he studied her face. "How much did you have to drink tonight?"

It dawned on Chad that she suddenly didn't seem as drunk as he'd originally thought.

She grinned. "Enough to give me the courage to make my proposal, but not enough that my head will hurt in the morning. I'm gonna have a clear head when we start our research."

Chad's heart sped up as she alluded to the three of them starting research...together.

Mercifully, Sean pulled his shit together and he was able to ask all the questions Chad couldn't seem to formulate.

"Research?"

Lauren looked at Sean and smiled. "You offered to be my Dom."

"You want me *and* Chad?"

"Chad too," Lauren said. She released Sean and stepped closer to Chad. He could barely detect the slightest trace of vodka on her breath, mixed with something so sweet he had to fight to remain still, instinct pushing him toward her for a taste.

"You're asking both of us to come to your bed?" Sean wasn't allowing for any misunderstandings.

"Both of you," she whispered. Then she surprised Chad by asking, "How come you never asked me out?"

Chad grasped for an answer and for a few foolish seconds, he thought perhaps he could do this. Could hop into bed with Lauren and Sean and everything would be fine.

"I beat him to the punch, Lauren." It was Sean who answered and Chad was grateful for his friend's interference.

"How did you beat him?" Lauren turned to look at Sean. "We were all friends for nearly four years before you approached me for a date. Four years," she stressed.

"We're too much alike, Lauren. I knew it would never work out." Chad's answer ranked up there with some of the biggest lies he'd ever told, but he thought it sounded plausible enough.

Lauren stared at him. "Do you want me, Chad?"

The word "yes" flew from him lips before he could

consider the consequences. Her face cleared and he realized Lauren hadn't been confident that her feelings for him would be returned. How could she not have known? "I've always wanted you."

Sean stepped forward. "So give us your proposal, Lauren. Lay it out like you said you were going to."

She moved to face both of them and she was steadier on her feet than Chad would have expected. It was clear her initial drunkenness had been at least fifty percent an act. "Three Sundays. Three days of submission. The three of us. We'll only play on Sundays. During the week, we'll go back to normal. Well, sort of normal. Sean, do you mind sleeping on the couch for a while?"

Sean shook his head. Chad was surprised by this friend's easy acceptance, but obviously all three of them knew things were about to change. Drastically.

Lauren continued explaining her suggestion. "By taking a week break in between each ménage experience, you'll have time to figure out if you want the Sundays to stretch into more. Because I'll tell you both now—I want more."

"A threesome?" Chad asked. "Forever?"

She nodded. "Oh, and I'll only submit if it's both of you...at the same time. No taking turns. Okay?"

Neither Chad nor Sean responded. Chad wanted to say "hell yes" to everything, but he knew deep in his heart this was a mistake. However, for once, he couldn't deny what he wanted. Lauren was offering him a dream and he wasn't strong enough to refuse it.

Sean was the first to break his silence, but his words to Lauren caught Chad off-guard. "Kiss him."

The second the words left Sean's lips, it felt as if all the air had been sucked out of the room.

"What?" Lauren blinked and Chad could tell she was suddenly nervous.

"I want you to kiss Chad. In front of me. I want to know you understand exactly what it is you're asking."

She shook her head, but something snapped inside Sean.

"Dammit, Lauren! If we do this, we're doing it right. You're used to Sean, the easygoing boyfriend, but now you've asked me to teach you about submission, about a ménage. That changes things. *Kiss him.* I missed the first one. I'm not missing any more."

"Sean," Lauren said, but Sean was on a roll.

"This isn't a game. I've agreed to your rules, agreed to try, to sleep on the couch, but I'm not going to be denied this. Do it."

"Listen, man," Chad started, surprised by the strength of Sean's voice, his needs. He'd never seen his friend so commanding, so powerful...so sexy.

"Shut up, Chad. It's time to stop talking. Goddamn it, all we ever do is talk and analyze. I've had enough. You're going to kiss Lauren and I'm watching you do it."

Sean's words provoked a strong reaction in him. His cock rose, tenting the front of his pants. "Fuck," Chad murmured, trying to adjust quickly, but his motions were too slow to hide his hungry response from Sean or Lauren.

"You have ten seconds to kiss him, Lauren."

"Or?"

Chad grinned at her cheeky question. She wasn't afraid or unwilling.

Sean gave her a wolfish grin. "Do you really want to know the answer to that question?"

His answer provoked something in Lauren, something that had clearly lay dormant, buried so deep in her psyche none of them had ever seen it. Now that Chad was witnessing it, he knew they were right to pursue this. He suspected the next three Sundays would change his entire life, though God only knew whether it would be for better or worse.

She took the few steps required to stand directly in front of him.

Sean had to make his own quick adjustment below the waist, the rough denim of his jeans less forgiving than Chad's loose trousers, and Chad grinned at the sight.

Chad looked at Sean one last time and, for the briefest moment, he was afraid his best friend could see the naked desire in his eyes.

"Do it," Sean urged again, and Chad responded, claiming Lauren's soft lips.

Chad kissed her as he'd always dreamed, grasping her waist firmly to him as their lips melted together. It was one of the most beautiful moments of his life and he suspected he'd never forget it. As the kiss advanced, grew hungrier and hotter, Lauren's arm wrapped around his shoulders and he pulled her closer.

. . .

SEAN'S LEGS went weak with the vision of his two best friends kissing and for the first time in his life, everything snapped into place.

As they broke apart, Chad and Lauren looked only at each other for several painfully long moments. Sean's heart beat rapidly as he waited for them to look at him. One glance—all he needed was one glance—and he'd know if he'd made the worst mistake of his life...or the smartest decision ever.

Lauren took a tiny step back and they both turned to look at him at the same time.

And Sean smiled.

"I need to go to bed," Lauren said shakily. Sean nodded. While it was physically painful to let her walk away, he suspected they would all be smart to take a night to consider what they were about to do.

"Good night," Chad said.

"Night," Lauren whispered as she walked out of the room.

Chad walked over to the couch and sat down. "What the fuck just happened?"

Sean dropped onto the recliner, feeling as shell-shocked as Chad looked. "We're having sex. The three of us."

"Bit more than just sex, Sean. She wants us to master her as well."

Sean blew out a long breath. "Yeah. I got that part,

believe me." He let his gaze travel over to meet Chad's. "You wanna do it, don't you?"

Chad nodded slowly. "More than I want my next breath, but we can't. I mean, this isn't something—"

"We're doing it."

Chad looked as if he'd been struck with a rock. "Jesus, Sean! You know, at some point you need to stop living your life on impulse. There are too many variables, too many potential problems that you aren't seeing. I don't think you understand—"

Sean cut him off, tired of listening to the talk, tired of analyzing the shit out of everything. "We're doing it."

CHAPTER SEVEN

Sean stood at the kitchen counter and poured water into the coffeemaker. He needed a jolt—or several—of caffeine if he was going to make it through the next few minutes without fucking up. He'd tossed and turned and jacked off all night as he lay on the couch thinking about Lauren's proposition and that damn kiss. She'd reached into his head, pulled out all his naughtiest fantasies and was now offering them to him on a silver platter.

The youngest of seven kids, he'd spent a good portion of his life watching his siblings fall in love, each of them finding their perfect relationship. He'd witnessed love in all forms take shape in his family and he'd certainly been impacted by what he'd seen. Throughout, he'd found himself most influenced by Keira's and Killian's relationships.

He'd spent years witnessing the silent, strong control Will exerted over his sister and he'd watched her blossom under it. The idea of offering Lauren the same escape, the same chance to be so much more than she realized she could be, was an exciting thought.

Chad cursed and Sean turned to see his friend wiping a hot splatter of bacon grease off his arm. They'd followed this same routine every Sunday for years—rising late and cooking up a big breakfast. The image of his best friend kissing his girl last night hovered again in his mind.

The fact that Sean had always clicked most with his older brother Killian, as well as K's best friend Justin, just proved how stupid he'd been not to consider the possibility of a ménage sooner. K and Justin lived in a threesome with Chad's sister. While it had taken years for Chad to truly come to terms with the idea of Lily living with two men, Sean had been fascinated, enthralled, even covetous of the relationship.

Like Justin and K, he and Chad had been best friends for a lifetime. While the opportunity to share the woman he loved with Chad was more exciting than he'd ever imagined, he was terrified too. What would it be like to lie in bed with Lauren *and* Chad?

His cock stirred, rising at the thought, and he grinned to himself.

Guess that answers that question.

It would be hot, sexy—perfect.

"Morning, sunshine," he heard Chad say behind him.

Sean turned to see Lauren walk into the kitchen. She was wearing the T-shirt and silky lounge pants she always slept in. His cock completed its journey to fully awake.

Her hair was sleep-tousled, her face slightly flushed. In a word, she was beautiful.

She gave them both a sweet smile. "You guys still talking to me?"

Sean tilted his head. "Why wouldn't we be?"

She shrugged. "I think I may have come on a little strong last night."

Chad pulled the bacon off the burner then leaned against the kitchen counter, crossing his arms over his chest. "Maybe so, but does the offer still stand?"

Lauren hesitated for only the briefest of moments before nodding once.

"Good," Sean said, walking around the island. He'd kept his hands to himself last night. Now, all bets were off. "Take off that shirt."

Her pink cheeks turned scarlet, but she didn't refuse him. Her hands simply grabbed the hem of her shirt and she pulled it over her head in one quick movement. She wasn't wearing a bra.

"Holy mother," he heard Chad murmur behind him.

Sean never took his eyes off Lauren's face. "You're gorgeous."

She smiled. "And you don't mess around."

He grinned and lifted his hand to cup one of her breasts in his palm. She gasped as his fingers tightened on her erect nipple. "I want you."

"Jesus Christ." Chad's continued muttering made him laugh.

"Are you going to keep evoking religion or are you gonna hop in here?" Sean asked.

"Goddamn it," Chad said, stepping closer. "I was hoping we could discuss this first."

Lauren shook her head. "I told you last night what I wanted. The rules haven't changed. Just the three of us together for the next three Sundays." Her gaze clung to Chad's and Sean could see how committed she was to her request. She wasn't hesitating, wasn't hedging or uncertain. She wanted them.

Sean bent forward until his lips were a breath away from hers. "Three Sundays. All of us. Together." He kissed her, using his tongue, his teeth to drive home his words. He was intensely aware of Chad stepping closer, his friend's hand grasping Lauren's other breast, their fingers bumping into each other as they played with her plump flesh. She was well endowed, her breasts full and firm.

Sean released her mouth, moving away a few inches so Chad could take a turn with her lips. He sucked in a deep breath as he watched their tongues touch. Drawn forward by some strange impulse, he leaned closer, nuzzling Lauren's cheek, felt Chad's breath hot on his face. The three of them were sharing the same space, the same air, and the temperature in the room seemed to rise a hundred degrees in an instant.

Lauren raised her arms, wrapping one around his neck, the other around Chad's. He reclaimed his grip on her breast, his knuckles brushing against Chad's as he held on to the other one.

"Get up on the table," Chad growled when he and Lauren's lips parted.

"Take your pants off first," Sean added.

Lauren laughed lightly. "Tsk, tsk, tsk. So impatient."

Sean's gaze narrowed. He knew the moment she'd made her proposal the sex between the three of them would be explosive. He'd also known she'd struggle with the control issue. He took a step back and Chad did the same.

One glance at his friend's face proved Chad shared his concern.

Lauren seemed confused by their retreat. "What's wrong?"

Chad crossed his arms over his chest. "I told you we needed to talk about this. Establish ground rules."

Suddenly Chad's earlier hesitance took on a different meaning and Sean gave his friend a guilty grin. Chad constantly gave him shit for diving into things without thinking them through.

"Ground rules?" Lauren asked.

Sean chuckled, but he wasn't really amused. "One ground rule. You do what we say, when we say."

His arrogant tone piqued her anger, just as he'd known it would. "Excuse me?" she said, her voice dripping with fury.

He stepped forward and put his hand under her chin, pushing her face up. The movement was premeditated. He was looming over her, using his height, his broad build to prove he was more than man enough to dominate her.

Her gaze shifted to Chad. He knew she was nervous when Chad stepped forward as well. They both had her by half a foot height-wise and at least a hundred pounds of sheer muscle.

"You agreed to submit to us. I told you this wouldn't be a game, that there would be no pretending, and you still said yes."

She nodded slowly. "The problem is I want to kill you when you use that obnoxious tone with me. Makes it sort of hard to submit."

Sean rubbed a hand over his face trying to hide his grin. God, he loved her. Loved her spunkiness, her feisty nature and her honesty.

When he spoke again, his voice was softer. "Lauren, I know you're used to being an equal in our relationship, but you asked us to teach you about submission, which means you need to let us call the shots. Trust us to take care of you and your needs."

She blew out a breath and nodded. "You're right. I did ask for it. It's just I've never let anyone dominate me in the bedroom. You know that. Before you, Sean, I was pretty much always the aggressor."

Chad laughed at her confession. "Little Dominatrix, eh? Shame you didn't pull that subject out of the hat. I think you'd rock a leather cat suit."

"Maybe if you boys are good, I'll let you see it." Sean shook his head and Lauren muttered, "Shit. Yeah, I'm defi-nitely gonna suck at this."

Chad wasn't discouraged. He took Lauren's hand as he pulled out a kitchen chair. "Sit there."

"What about my pants?" she asked seductively as Chad gently pushed her down.

"Later."

Sean watched Chad walk over to the pantry, pulling down an apron from the hook on the door. "The way I see it," Chad said as he walked toward her, "you've got too much freedom right now. Maybe we should start these lessons with something easy."

Chad grasped Lauren's hands and pulled them behind her back, tying them together with the apron strings.

Lauren's nipples tightened and her breathing accelerated. Sean grinned at his friend's ingenuity and patience.

Sean stepped forward as Chad checked the binding.

"Bondage is easier?" Lauren asked as Chad moved to stand beside him.

Chad nodded. "Limits your freedom."

"I can still talk," she teased.

Sean laughed. It was their first time together and no doubt they were all equal parts nervous and excited. Lauren talked when she was anxious. "Not for long," he murmured.

Taking a deep breath, he unbuttoned his jeans and pulled down the zipper. The room was quiet and Sean tried to keep his hand steady as two sets of eyes watched his every move.

Glancing from Lauren to Chad, Sean saw his friend watching him, his face implacable, unreadable. Lauren's was a bit easier to decipher. She was eager, ready. He pulled his cock free, suppressing a groan of relief as the tight denim had been quickly crossing from uncomfortable to painful.

"Sean," Lauren whispered. He took a step closer as she licked her lips.

"All you have to do is say stop, Lauren. If it's too much or you get scared, just say stop and we will. That's where the trust comes in."

She nodded slowly. "What will you do if I say go, go, go?"

He wanted to laugh. She was funny, adventurous, the perfect fit. Unfortunately, his body wasn't supplying enough blood to his brain to allow him to remember anything except his cock.

One more step. Just one more and he was there, directly in front of her. She opened her mouth and took him in. He couldn't have held back the groan that escaped his lips if his life had depended on it. He reached down and took her face in his hands. Her eyes met his and he knew he'd found paradise when she sucked the head of his cock harder, deeper.

From the corner of his eye, he saw Chad shift slightly so he could watch. Chad's hand was moving and Sean knew he'd undone his own pants and was rubbing his erection.

Sean pulled out and took a step to the side, making room for his friend. "Suck Chad's cock," he said, his voice so deep and husky, he barely recognized it as his own.

"Yes," she whispered. She squeezed her legs together and Sean marveled at how much this act, an act that was about to bring him to his knees, was turning her on too.

She took Chad's cock in her mouth and Sean stood there, spellbound. His friend was a bit longer than him but not quite as thick. He realized he could've stood there watching the erotic tableau before him all day.

Chad began to thrust into her mouth faster. His friend's hands tightened in Lauren's hair and she closed her eyes with need. Unable to stop himself, Sean knelt beside her, wanting to be closer.

"Suck him harder, Lauren," Sean instructed. "Run your tongue along the bottom, pay attention to that little soft spot just under the head."

Lauren was obeying Sean's instructions. He heard Chad groan as Lauren followed his commands. Her movements were pulling his friend closer to the brink.

"I can't hold off," Chad said, the words sounding as if they'd been pulled from his chest, and Lauren sucked even harder. "Goddamn it."

"He's ready now. So close," Sean said, reaching up and running a loving hand through her hair. "You're incredible, Lauren. Now," Sean said, the word triggering Chad's climax. As he watched his friend come, he whispered, "Swallow it. Drink it all down."

Sean closed his eyes and leaned forward to kiss Lauren's cheek softly...then turned his face slightly so his nose brushed briefly against Chad's cock, drawn to the scent of his friend's arousal.

Chad gasped as he backed away, pulling out of Lauren's mouth. Sean's eyes flew open but he saw only Lauren, smiling at him. It was clear she hadn't noticed anything amiss.

Sean braced himself to face his friend. He glanced up, saw a look of confusion on Chad's face. Better that than the anger he'd expected. He wanted to say he was sorry, but he wasn't. Chad took another step away...and it was Sean's temper that flared.

"My turn," he said, rising from where he was kneeling. Sean moved, edging Chad out of the way. If his friend was still determined to fight their attraction to each other, then so be it. He wasn't about to lose one minute of this time with Lauren.

He ran his finger along Lauren's lower lip but didn't step closer. He knew this day was supposed to be about dominance and submission and he wanted to make sure it initiated her into the lifestyle properly. But he'd spent too many nights in Lauren's bed. They'd established too many comfortable patterns that were hard to break. He didn't want to scare her, but God knew he couldn't pull any punches now. He was standing on a precipice and what he did now could potentially leave him facing a future without her, without Chad.

Lauren leaned forward and ran her tongue along his erect cock. "Please," she whispered.

Her words were his undoing and he pushed his cock into her mouth faster than usual, not stopping until he felt the back of her throat. He expected her to pull away, gag, revolt. She did none of those things. She pushed him farther in and swallowed.

The reins slipped from his grasp. He placed his hands on the side of her head, holding her still until her gaze rose to meet his. He saw Chad step to the side, knew his friend was getting a better view of what he was doing.

Sean waited, watched her closely for some sign of distress, some signal that it was too much. "I want to fuck your mouth."

She released a small sound that couldn't be misconstrued as anything other than consent. Her body relaxed and she bent her head farther, inviting him to take her deeper.

Sean began to move and she welcomed his quick, hard thrusts. He was taking her rougher than he'd ever dared. He was fucking Lauren's mouth. And she was loving it. *He* was loving it.

He turned to look at Chad. His friend's eyes never drifted from Lauren's mouth, from his cock. Sean felt a rush of more blood filling his already painful erection. Lauren moaned but adjusted quickly.

One look below Chad's waist told Sean his friend was recovering from his previous climax in record time. Sean also knew he was rapidly approaching the point of no return.

"God," he cried out, thrusting harder. Chad stepped behind Lauren's chair, stooping to untie her hands. His friend's gaze never left Sean's cock fucking her mouth.

Then Chad surprised him. He bent down behind

Lauren's chair and whispered something to her. Sean couldn't hear the words over the roaring in his ears that signaled his coming climax. Lauren's eyes drifted shut when Chad's fingers reached around the chair to play with her breasts. He'd encaged her upper body with his arms, his chest replacing the binding he'd just released.

Unable to hold back, Sean came, a litany of groans and praises and professions of love falling from his lips.

When he came to his senses, he realized that throughout his orgasm, he hadn't been looking at Lauren— but at Chad.

Chad had been looking at him, too.

And worst of all...so had Lauren.

One look at her face told him he'd revealed too much. One look and he knew he'd given himself away once and for all. There had been times in the past when he thought she'd seen, thought she'd noticed, but he'd fought hard to hide the truth. Now, with one look, everything had been revealed.

He'd hurt her.

Fuck.

With one look.

AS SEAN PULLED AWAY from her, Lauren's mind reeled and she was struck by the realization that her body and her heart were running in opposite directions.

She rubbed her legs together again. She'd never felt so hot and needy from giving a blowjob. While Sean took a couple steps away, obviously still trying to recover from his orgasm, Chad rubbed her shoulders, soothing *her* as much as her muscles. Her wits felt as if they were in tatters around her.

She knew the secret now. The thing that had eluded her for years. She'd always had a sense of some deeper connection between Sean and Chad, though not necessarily this. They'd been good at hiding it.

Sean was in love with Chad. How could she have been so blind?

Chad helped her stand and his face told her he knew what she'd seen. "Today is about you, Lauren. Only you. I swear."

Tears gathered at her eyes and she wondered if that was true. She shook her head to show him she didn't believe it. Nothing that happened between the three of them would be *just* about her. It couldn't be. God, she'd never be so selfish, so self-absorbed.

Sean's face. She closed her eyes against the image of him right now. Fuck. His face as he looked at Chad was beautiful and tortured. She'd never seen such a combination. While she wanted to latch onto Chad's words and hold them close, her heart knew that would be too easy. And suddenly nothing about this was easy. There was too much history between Chad and Sean. Too many unspoken, unrequited feelings.

She'd been a fool to listen to Riley's advice. She'd thought she was engaging in a ménage, exploring some wicked fantasies. With her stupid plan, she'd blown the lid off an ancient, unseen volcano and she had a feeling they were all about to be taken down in the ensuing scorching lava flow.

"We're not stopping," Chad insisted. "A deal's a deal." Lauren wondered at Chad's sudden insistence. He'd been the most resistant to her proposal. He gripped the waistband of her lounge pants and pulled them down. She felt numb, uncertain, aroused beyond belief. He held her arm as she stepped out of them. Grasping her hips, he lifted her onto the kitchen table and pushed her to her back.

"Only you." He repeated those two words as he spread her legs apart and bent. His mouth took her pussy with a hunger she'd never experienced. There was no hesitation. No preliminaries or build up. He simply leaned over and fucked the hell out of her with his lovely mouth.

His tongue swiped at her, starting at her ass and moving up to her mons. When he found her clit, he brought his teeth into the play, nipping at the distended flesh until she was thrashing against the table.

"Shhhh." Sean's soft voice came from above her head. She wondered when he'd moved. As he touched her, she gave up her untoward thoughts.

Keira's words about submitting to Will drifted back to her. *He's shown me how to clear my mind, how to trust and love and feel. Believe me, after a night in his arms, I wake up every morning refreshed and ready to take on the world again.*

One day. She'd promised them this day to explore. She'd have an entire week to stress out about and try to sort through the rest. For now, she just wanted to give herself to the two men she loved more than life itself.

Sean's hands captured her wrists, pulling them against the tabletop, holding her firmly. The feeling of being trapped, helpless, increased her arousal and she groaned, feeling more moisture escape her pussy.

Chad noticed too; she saw him glance up at her face before he looked at Sean. "Bondage," he said. "She's into it. Big time."

Sean chuckled and tightened his grip. "I've got a book on Kinbaku. I think next week we should explore Japanese rope bondage."

"God," Lauren cried, thrusting her hips up, trying to get Chad's mouth on her body.

Chad pressed her hips down, holding her still.

"Fuck me," she demanded. "Please. You're killing me."

Chad didn't move. His eyes narrowed, his gaze darkened. Shit. So much for handing over control.

"You don't get it, do you, Lauren?" he asked before looking at Sean. "Help me turn her over."

Before she could grasp their intent, she was facedown, her upper body flat against the table while her legs hung over the edge, her feet on the floor.

Sean's hands were holding her shoulders firmly. He bent forward, pressing a soft kiss to her cheek before whispering in her ear, "Do you know what happens to naughty girls?"

She wanted to make some smartass comment, but held her tongue.

"No?" he asked. "Well, I'll tell you. They get spanked."

Chad ran his hand along her bare bottom. "How about we make things interesting?"

Lauren trembled from the impact of their touches, their taunts. She wouldn't make it much longer.

"Interesting?" she asked, her voice weak from her arousal.

"I read your research notes," Chad confessed. "Last night after you went to bed."

She sucked in a deep breath and held it. While she had to study her ass off for her four-point-oh, Chad was a natural student. He was exceedingly bright with a photographic memory. He was also very good at seeing through people's words, to the heart of the matter. It was one of the reasons she suspected he'd be an amazing psychologist.

"Okay," she said, dragging out the word. She had a pretty good idea what her notes had revealed, what secret, well-hidden fantasy he'd discovered.

Sean's hands tightened briefly on her shoulders and she could tell Chad had captured his friend's undivided attention. "What did they say? What does she want?"

"To be captured. Forced." Chad whispered the words, but they struck Lauren like a lightning bolt.

"God, yes," Sean hissed, his hands releasing her.

Her body was on fire, from excitement *and* embarrassment. Slowly she pushed herself up from the table, wondering how far she would get if she tried to run. Her gaze slid to the door and Sean laughed.

"Try it. Bet you don't get your big toe into the hallway."

She stood up straight and threw her shoulders back. Despite her nudity, she refused to hide her face. "Why on earth would I run? For your information, I've been trying to hook up with you two forever." As she spoke, her actions belied her words. She pulled on her lounge pants. She needed to get the hell out of here.

Neither man moved to stop her as she picked up her T-shirt and put it on again as well. "You know, I don't appreciate you looking at my stuff, Chad. I don't go through your research notes and jump to false conclusions."

Chad grinned and she got a sense he was patronizing her. "Nothing false about what I said. Admit it, Lauren. You want to be chased, held down. You want us to force you to do all sorts of naughty things and then to force orgasm after orgasm on you. Think of the adrenaline rush."

Her breathing suddenly became labored and she was struggling to get enough air into her lungs.

She wanted exactly what he said and more.

She glanced at Sean. One look at his predatory gaze and she knew he did too.

She turned and sprinted for the door. She'd obviously caught them by surprise or they were giving her a head start, because neither man immediately started to chase her. As she reached the top of the stairs, she heard them coming.

"You may as well give up, Lauren," Sean taunted. "We're going to find you."

She dashed down the hallway to Chad's bathroom, raced inside and paused. Peering out the door, she saw both men walk into her bedroom. Using the connecting door between the bathroom and Chad's room, she tiptoed past his bed, tucking herself behind his dresser.

The men approached the bathroom. She would have to time her escape just right if she hoped to be able to make it down the stairs again. Her heart was rushing, her blood pulsing...her pussy gushing. She'd always fantasized about this, but the reality was so much more intense, exciting.

"Come out, come out, wherever you are," Chad teased.

"Come out and we'll let you come," Sean added. "Make us catch you and you're gonna suffer first."

Sean's words were almost enough to prod her from her spot. Then she grinned. Nope, they were working for their reward. Judging from their voices, she could tell they were both in the bathroom. Moving fast, she darted out Chad's bedroom door and ran down the stairs.

Footsteps pounding behind her proved she'd just about run out of time.

She'd reached the front foyer when someone grabbed her from behind, gripping her hair tightly. The pain in her scalp sent an overwhelming impulse straight to her cunt. She was dripping wet.

She stopped suddenly and kicked her leg behind her, connecting with a shin. The grip on her hair loosened and she heard Sean curse. She laughed and started to run again, but Chad was on her in an instant. Careful of her kicking legs, he shoved her forward until she was pressed firmly face-first against the hallway wall. She struggled in his arms, not ready to give up the fight.

Reaching over her shoulder, she tried to grab a handful of Chad's hair. He captured her wrist, pulling it behind her back, his grip tight, painful, sexy as hell. She'd never been so turned on in her life.

He repeated the same motion with her other hand, using the pressure of his hold on her wrists to keep her pinned to the wall. "Surrender," he said.

"Never." She tried to twist out of his hold, though she knew she'd been captured.

"Submit." Sean's voice sounded next to her.

She turned her head and looked into the face of her friend, her boyfriend, the man she would have sworn she knew better than herself. She blinked quickly, the blinders falling away.

She'd never seen the real Sean before this day.

She wanted him. Wanted the dominant, controlling sex-on-legs man standing before her. She'd never thought their sex life anything other than incredible, but now she found herself resenting the things he'd been withholding, the wasted time.

"It's not a game, Lauren," Sean said, and for the first time, she understood.

"I know," she whispered.

Chad's grip slackened but he didn't release her wrists. He pulled her away from the wall and propelled her toward the living room. She was breathing heavily, from the running, the thrill of the chase, the fear of the unknown.

Once they entered the room, Chad released her. She stood in the center of the space, watching him.

"Take off those clothes," Chad growled.

Hastily, she removed her T-shirt and pants, silently rejoicing when they moved to do the same.

When they were all naked, Chad sat on the edge of the recliner and crooked his finger at her. "Come here."

She obeyed. They'd captured her. They'd gained her surrender.

As she approached, Chad reached for her right hand, used it to pull her facedown over his lap. She didn't have time to consider her vulnerable position before his hand came down against the naked flesh of her ass. She cried out and tried to push up, but Chad's grip was strong, immovable.

He slapped her bare bottom four more times, using more strength than she would have expected.

She sensed Sean moving directly behind her. As he knelt, his hands pushed her legs apart, his chest brushed against her sore ass.

Without preamble he thrust two fingers into her pussy and this time, she cried out—from surprise and relief.

"Is she wet?" Chad asked.

"Soaking." Sean thrust his fingers several times more before pulling out. Glancing over her shoulder, she watched Sean sit back, giving Chad more room to move while maintaining his own bird's eye view of her bare ass.

Chad moved in, continuing to spank her, and she jerked as his hand landed on her already sore ass.

When he stopped, Sean moved to her side and picked up the motion. Sean's spanking differed from Chad's. He operated on the quantity-rather-than-quality concept. While Sean's strikes weren't as hard, there were lots of them, coming faster than she could count. Her ass was on fire but she couldn't deny the heat was moving inward, creeping along her body and sending sparks to her pussy. She'd never been more aroused—or confused—in her life.

When the spanking stopped, their hands became softer and gentler as they stroked her, touched her, tantalized her.

Sean pushed his fingers inside her pussy. "So hot," he murmured.

Chad's finger teased the opening to her ass. They both reached beneath her to pinch her taut nipples while she squirmed on Chad's lap like a worm on a hook.

Then, abruptly, it all stopped.

She quivered from a need greater than she'd ever known. "God, please," she said, her voice breaking slightly.

"Shhh," Chad murmured. "Let us take care of you, sunshine."

His kind words were almost her undoing as the past few minutes caught up with her. Too many things descended on her at once and she started to shake. Her mind and her body felt trapped in a vortex of emotions. They'd kept her on the verge of an orgasm for too long and if she didn't come soon, she thought she might go insane.

"Hey," Sean said, lightly caressing her sore bottom

before rising. "Come here." He lifted her from Chad's lap and carried her to the couch. Chad followed and sat on the coffee table as Sean stretched over Lauren's trembling body.

He pushed inside her, filling her in an instant, and a sigh of relief escaped. Chad chuckled softly, moving to kneel by her head on the couch. Turning her face with a gentle hand against her cheek, he kissed her as Sean slowly and leisurely made love to her.

She was on birth control—she and Sean had long ago dispensed with using condoms. She knew she wouldn't want anything between her and Chad as well. Sean's lips engulfed her breast, his tongue teasing the flesh there as he slowly, deeply thrust inside her. The combination of Sean's and Chad's lips on her body, along with Sean's lovemaking, threw her into an orgasm so powerful she couldn't believe she wasn't shaking the rafters of the house.

Sean followed her, his climax coming faster than usual. Obviously she wasn't the only one affected by the power of the moment.

She wasn't given time to recover as Sean pulled out and Chad took his place. He paused, his cock poised at the entrance of her body, and she knew why he was waiting.

"I want you," she whispered. "Just you. Nothing between us."

He smiled and pushed into her with a strength she should have expected, given his spanking technique. Chad's lovemaking was completely different from Sean's, harder, hungrier. While she and Sean had years to try to sate their desire for each other, Chad had been waiting... and watching. He drove her to the brink with his sheer brute strength. The speed of his thrusts took her breath away. Chad was managing to find hot buttons she didn't know she possessed, pushing her toward her orgasm with hard strokes and sexy, dirty words murmured in her ear.

When she came again it was just as hard, just as potent as the first, and Chad came with her, collapsing over her body, caging her beneath his smooth, firm flesh.

"Holy shit," she muttered after several moments.

She opened her eyes to find Sean sitting on the coffee table looking at them, looking as star-struck as she felt. "You have no idea how hot it is watching you two fuck."

She smiled. "You'll have to describe it for me later. I was too busy coming to concentrate on anything else."

Chad rose slowly and she moaned as he pulled free of her body. "Sore?" he asked, his voice laced with concern.

"Everywhere," she said. "And I love it."

Sean laughed and glanced at the clock on the DVR. "It's only ten a.m."

She narrowed her eyes. "So?"

"So Sunday is still young."

CHAPTER EIGHT

Sean lay on the couch with Lauren tucked in front of him. Chad sprawled out on the floor with his back resting again the couch, his hand lazily drifting along Lauren's naked thigh.

After their adventure in the living room, they'd polished off the biggest breakfast in history, devouring a pound of bacon, a dozen scrambled eggs and a mess of hash browns. They'd decided to eat naked, laughing and caressing throughout the entire meal until they were all so aroused, they'd cleared off the kitchen table and indulged in round two.

Lauren stretched, giving a contented sigh.

"Still okay?" Sean asked.

Chad was amazed by her resilience, her intense sexuality. They had pushed her hard, withholding her orgasms for ages, before finally taking turns inside her sweet body again.

"Mmm hmm." She hummed her assent. "Little tired. Lot sweaty."

Chad grinned. "A shower sounds good."

"A shower sounds great," Sean concurred.

Lauren shook her head. "Jacuzzi tub. We've been so busy with classes, unpacking and working, we've never used it."

Sean stood up and took her hand, helping her rise. "Come on. I'll start the water."

The three of them climbed the stairs, stopping for long kisses and teasing touches. Chad followed them to the master bathroom, feeling for the first time since they'd moved into this house as if he wasn't an outsider.

Sean started the water, steam quickly filling the room. Lauren rummaged around under the sink, pulling out some girlie shower stuff.

"Jasmine," she said, opening the bottle and adding some to the water. "Smells nice."

"I'm gonna smell like a chick," Sean said, crinkling his nose at the scent.

Chad laughed, joking, "Might be a welcome change to the way you smell right now."

"Hey," Sean said with feigned affront. "We've been doing quite a workout down there."

Lauren climbed into the tub and sighed as she sank into the hot water. "Ahh. Heaven. I think I'm going to have to look into joining a gym if I hope to keep up with you guys for two more Sundays. I'm obviously too out of shape for this."

Chad grinned, joining her in the water. When he was seated, he reached for her, pulling her back against his front, nestling her between his legs. She lounged with him, grasping his hands to wrap them around her stomach.

"You're doing just fine, gorgeous," Chad murmured, kissing her cheek.

Sean took his place on the opposite side of the tub, sinking down until his head was completely submerged.

Chad and Lauren laughed when Sean disappeared for several seconds. When he reemerged, he shook his head like a dog, pelting them with water.

"Hey!" Lauren laughed, throwing her hands up to deflect the large drops splashing in her eyes.

Sean gave them a shit-eating grin before moving to his knees and crawling forward. He didn't stop until his face reached Lauren's and he gave her a long, wet kiss. Chad marveled over how natural their closeness felt. He'd always been a firm believer in personal space...but Lauren and Sean *fit* in his space. He raised his hand to touch Sean's hair as he kissed Lauren, before stopping in mid-air.

He was about to caress Sean.

He dropped his hand quickly, checking to see if Sean or Lauren had noticed. They hadn't. Their eyes were closed.

Chad swallowed heavily. He'd nearly touched Sean. He'd *wanted* to touch Sean.

He tried to shake off that unwanted realization. Clearly it was just the heat of the moment. It was fucking with his head, making him think of certain things...things he'd tried to repress for years.

After Lauren issued her proposal, he'd spent most of the night tossing and turning, considering all the pros and cons of accepting her offer. When his considerations had led him to a draw, he'd gotten up and starting reading her research notes. It was her words, the secret fantasies she'd revealed in her writing, that finally convinced him to take the chance, the gift she was giving them.

Now he was questioning that decision. Being with Lauren was a dream come true. Unfortunately, that dream was coming with a price. He'd known being close to Sean like this would be hard. He just didn't realize how hard.

Finally, Sean and Lauren parted. Chad reached over and picked up the soap. Working up a lather in his hands, he rubbed the sweet-smelling suds over her skin, enjoying the pink flush of arousal that painted it as he touched her. Sean joined in the washing, massaging Lauren's breasts, toying with her tight nipples as Chad ventured lower, running his fingers through the trimmed hair of her pussy before working two inside.

Lauren squirmed between them, her need growing quickly. They'd driven her to countless orgasms already today and yet, she never failed to respond to more.

The firm clenching of her inner muscles alerted him to her approaching climax, but Sean surprised him by grasping his wrist and stopping him from driving her over the top.

"Wait," Sean said. Chad remained motionless, trying

not to acknowledge the fact Sean was still holding on to him or the fact that his friend's simple touch had driven even more blood to his far-too-full erection.

"Not this way," Sean said. He released his grip on Chad's hand and moved back. Rising out of the water, he perched on the edge of the tub. Chad's gaze landed on his friend's large cock, hard and ready to roll.

In their previous encounters, he'd avoided looking at Sean as much as possible, trying instead to concentrate of Lauren. Now Sean sat before them in all his beautiful glory and Chad couldn't have averted his eyes for all the money in the world.

"Come here, Lauren," Sean instructed. "I want you to suck my cock while Chad fucks you from behind."

Chad closed his eyes and prayed he'd be able to make it inside Lauren's body without embarrassing himself. He was too worked up, too horny. Fuck, it was as if Sean was crawling around inside his head. The entire day had been too overwhelming, too hot, too fucking incredible.

Lauren quickly moved to her knees, crawling between Sean's legs. She grasped his friend's cock, running her hand up and down the turgid flesh with a firm, strong grip that left Sean visibly gritting his teeth. She did everything right. Chad knew that from experience. She bent down and took Sean into her mouth.

"Jesus, man," Sean muttered. "Get inside her. This isn't gonna take long."

Chad grinned. "Thank God."

He pushed inside her from behind, no preamble, no

foreplay. He could see from the strained expression on his friend's face he wasn't joking. He hadn't thrust more than a handful of times before Lauren's climax began, her orgasm milking his cock in a way that was almost painful.

"Fuck," he groaned. Two more strokes in that tight, wet heat and it would be all over. Lauren must've sensed he was close. She released Sean's cock, her fingers drifting down to play with his balls. She cupped them and Sean moaned.

Chad couldn't take his eyes off her actions, his friend's reactions. He was riveted to the spot, to this moment.

Sean's hand tangled in Lauren's hair, his other gripping his cock. He lifted her head up so she could see his face and Chad followed her gaze, gasped at the dominance written in every line of his friend's face. He'd never seen Sean so controlling, so powerful. It was the most amazing thing he'd ever seen.

"You ready?" Sean asked, his husky tone proving he wouldn't be denied exactly what he wanted.

Lauren's pussy clenched with excitement and Chad couldn't restrain his groan. He was a goner.

"Yes," she whispered.

"Good," Sean said, pushing her head toward his lap, guiding his cock between her open lips. "Suck me hard."

Lauren took him into her mouth but Sean retained control of her movements, using his hand in her hair to drive her at the pace he wanted.

Lauren's reactions let Chad know exactly how much she loved Sean's rough treatment, and he realized he was fighting a losing battle. Gripping her hips, he gave in to his own needs, pushing inside her harder than he'd ever fucked a woman before. Faster. Deeper. He felt her climax begin but he refused to stop, refused to give her even a moment's relief as he thrust over and over.

Her climax continued, one giving way to another continuously until Chad heard Sean's cry. He knew from his friend's jerky hold on Lauren's head that he was coming. Shooting his come down her throat. For a moment Chad imagined he could taste the salty offering himself, and it was that thought that pushed him into the hardest, most painful, most satisfying orgasm of his life.

It wasn't until they'd gotten out of the bathtub, dried off, and begun to fall into an exhausted sleep in the king-sized bed in the master bedroom that the truth crashed in on him.

Chad stared at the ceiling in the bedroom, the sounds of Lauren's and Sean's breathing taunting him as he realized just how fucked he really was. This was their bed, their room. He couldn't stay for long. Not without losing the battle he'd waged for a lifetime.

Three Sundays. Just three. And then he'd find a way to forge a new future...one without Sean and Lauren. One without his heart.

LAUREN WATCHED Chad pull out of the driveway from the front window. They'd dozed all afternoon, the three of them exhausted from so much sex. When they woke up, Chad volunteered to run out for Chinese. All of them were starving but no one had the energy to cook.

Sean walked up behind her, wrapping his arms around her waist.

"You ready to talk about it?" she asked.

Sean sighed heavily. "I should've known you wouldn't leave it alone."

She turned in his arms and gave him a sad smile. "All these years. Why didn't you ever tell me?" She tried to hide the hurt in her voice but knew she'd failed.

Sean rested his forehead against hers, closed his eyes. "You really didn't know?"

She sighed. When she'd first seen Sean's face in the kitchen, she'd been shocked. Now she suspected there'd always been an inkling, an awareness, deep inside. She shrugged and grinned. "I'm not sure. Maybe I sensed it. I don't know. I'm in love with you. I think maybe that made me blind to a lot of things that should have been obvious." She felt a slight pang as another thought occurred to her. "Did you think you couldn't tell me?"

He shook his head quickly. "No. Hell no. I didn't say anything because talking about it wouldn't have changed anything. Chad's not interested. Let's just leave it at that."

"How do you know? Have you ever told him how you feel?"

Sean released his hold on her and turned away, walking toward the living room. "Dammit, Lauren. Can you please drop this? It's not gonna happen. Ever. I would think you'd be more interested in talking about the ménage we all just jumped into this morning."

She followed him to the living room, quickly claiming the spot next to him on the couch. He wasn't escaping this conversation. He'd spent years running away from the truth, lying to her, to Chad. She couldn't quite believe that her best friend, her boyfriend, the man she'd planned to spend her life with, had hidden such a big secret from her.

"The whole ménage issue is moot until your feelings for Chad are resolved. Surely you know that. You're in love with him."

Sean started to deny it, she could see it in his face. Then he simply shrugged. "Doesn't matter. He doesn't feel the same."

"You know that for a fact?"

Sean nodded. "Yeah. I do."

His answer took Lauren aback. She was so sure he'd been hiding his feelings from Chad as well. To know that he'd told Chad shook her. Had she been runner-up? All these years, had she simply been Sean's second choice after Chad rejected him. "Oh." She turned her head, blinking rapidly. She wouldn't let Sean see her cry. She couldn't.

"Jesus, Lauren. God, baby, don't do that." Sean's arms engulfed her, triggering the tears she'd been trying to hide. "It's not what you think. Christ, I'm goofy, head-over-heels in love with you. How in the hell can you doubt that?"

"I don't," she said, sniffling. She turned and buried her head in his all-too-comforting chest. "I just didn't know I was second choice."

"What the fuck?" Sean gripped her face, pulling it away from him. She was embarrassed to have him see the tears falling down her cheeks. "Are you nuts? I want you to listen to me and I want these words make their way into that thick skull of yours. You are, and always have been, my *only* choice. I met you and every other woman faded into the background."

"Woman," she whispered.

His scowl grew but she'd stumped him. She could see it. "I don't know how to say this so you'll understand. I want you. Want to spend the rest of my life with you. I want the same thing with Chad. And it doesn't have a damn thing to do with me settling for you or him rejecting me. My heart loves you both...just the same. It's never been a fucking competition. It's just been..."

His words faltered, but she didn't need to hear the rest.

Sean had just described her own emotions to a tee.

"I get it," she said. She grasped his wrists, his hands still cradling her face. "I feel the same way."

He looked at her, studied her face, and she saw the lines of tension around his eyes and mouth relax. "I know you do. It's Chad whose heart lies firmly in one camp. Yours."

Lauren considered the morning, remembered all they had done. While Sean's feelings for Chad had been simple to read, there had been moments when she'd seen a slight crack in Chad's shell as well. "I'm not so sure about that."

Sean scoffed. "Trust me on this, Lauren. He's in love with you. And only you."

She shook her head. "No." She really didn't believe that was true. While Sean had clearly expressed his interest in Chad before, she knew it hadn't been recently. Definitely not since they'd been dating. So, that meant his declaration had come years ago. Long enough for Chad's feelings to change. "I think you should approach the subject again."

"Forget it," Sean said quickly. "Not about to take another punch off that fucker. He hits hard."

Lauren was shocked. "He hit you?"

Sean shrugged. "I had it coming."

Lauren recalled the night she and Chad had confessed to kissing. Chad had been ready for Sean to hit him. It had almost seemed to her Chad had *wanted* Sean to throw a punch. Was he seeking penance for a blow he now regretted throwing?

"You have to talk to Chad again. How can we consider pursuing a lifetime as a threesome with you harboring these feelings?"

Sean fell silent as he considered her words. "I can't, Lauren. I'm sorry."

"Why not?"

He smiled sadly at her. "What if he still feels the same way? I've worked hard for years to put those feelings aside. If I tell him they're still there, he may leave. No." Sean shook his head. "He *will* leave."

Lauren felt her chest constrict with the pain of that thought. She fought to find some words of comfort, but she couldn't. The idea of Chad walking away from them paralyzed her with fear and she understood Sean's reticence.

Sean wrapped his arm around her shoulders. "And if he leaves, I'll lose you too."

"No," she said, refuting his words.

He placed his hand on her cheek. "Yes. You may not physically leave, but emotionally. Face it, it'll tear us both apart if Chad walks away from this."

"So, we can't let him leave," she said.

We can't let him leave.

CHAPTER NINE

"Well, that pizza place is a keeper," Killian said, leaning back and rubbing his stomach.

Lauren laughed as all the men in the room assumed a similar pose. Lily had invited Sean, Chad and her to join them for a little sweet Thursday relief at their place, and they'd wanted to try a new pizza shop that had opened in the area. Justin and Killian had started the sweet Thursday concept when they were in the Army. They liked to start the weekend a day early. The idea had stuck and Lauren had been invited to more than a few of these "not quite the weekend" get-togethers over the years.

Lily stood and started to clear up the paper plates and empty boxes. Lauren rose as well. "I'll help you," she offered, when the big screen TV flashed on.

"Hockey game," Killian announced. "I've got twenty bucks riding on this game with Tris."

Sean looked at his older brother and laughed. "You

too? That stupid bastard really thinks the Rangers are gonna pull out an upset. I told him he was crazy."

Killian rubbed his hands together. "Gonna be fun taking his money from him tomorrow."

Lauren rolled her eyes. The Collins men were infamous for their wagers. She wasn't sure if it was a side effect of being Irish or owning a pub, but it seemed no man in the family was immune.

"Come on, Lauren," Lily said. "As the testosterone rises in the room, so does the cussing, yelling and volume on the TV. I've got a bottle of wine in the kitchen that should help dull our senses."

"Sounds like an invitation I can't refuse." She turned around and looked at the guys lounging on the couch and in the two recliners. "You guys okay for beer?"

Chad raised his bottle. "I just set us all up with a round so we're good to go. Thanks."

She followed Lily to the kitchen, both of them loaded down with trash. They dumped it and Lauren claimed a chair at the table while Lily poured them both a glass of wine.

Lauren had been trying to work up the nerve to call Lily all week. Sunday's "research" had solidified a couple things in her mind. One, Lauren was deeply, truly, madly in love with Chad and Sean, and two, she wanted to make a lifetime of their relationship. She still hadn't given up hope that Chad and Sean would work out their issues, though God only knew how they would do that. She knew Sean intended to keep silent about his true feelings for his best friend, but she suspected the truth would come out eventually. When it did, she was prepared to do whatever it took to calm the waters. She wouldn't give up her men without one hell of a fight.

As for herself, there was one niggling worry that wouldn't let her go.

Lauren looked at Chad's sister and marveled over how little they resembled each other. Lily's dark hair and eyes were in direct contrast to Chad's dirty blond hair and blue eyes. If anything, Lily favored Sean more. Lily joined her at the table and she took a deep breath before asking the question that wouldn't leave her alone. "What do the people at work think about your lifestyle?"

If Lily was surprised by Lauren's discussion topic, she didn't give it away. She shrugged lightly. "I don't know. I've been with Justin and K for years now. I think my colleagues were probably a bit shocked at first when they realized I was living with two men. I have no doubt I was the subject of gossip for a while. However, human nature always wins out in the end. Those who were appalled pulled away, and those who were indifferent accepted it and ultimately forgot to be shocked. It hasn't affected how I do my work, so my bosses don't mention it."

"Are your neighbors okay with it?"

Lily nodded. "We're very good friends with our neigh-bors. Occasionally we babysit for Jules." Lily pointed to indicate Jules lived to the right. "She's going through a tough divorce and sometimes she needs a break. Gonna be hard for her, raising three rambunctious boys by herself, but that was a welcome alternative to doing it with an abusive alcoholic."

Lauren nodded. "And she's okay leaving her kids here? How does she explain there are two guys living with you?"

Lily laughed softly. "Her kids are all under the age of eight and I'm fairly certain she doesn't go into much detail about our sleeping arrangements. Besides, as I said, they're all boys and they love it here because they have two grown men to pitch them baseballs, toss around a football and wrestle with. Those boys love Justin and K. They're kids, and kids tend to like adults who are genuinely nice."

"Yeah," Lauren said. "That's true. And your family is okay with it? I mean, I know Killian's pop understands, but do your parents?"

Lily took a sip of her wine and frowned. "Do my parents understand?" Lily shook her head. "No. I don't think they do. However, they love me and so they've accepted it. As I said, time has made things easier. Justin and Killian have gone with me to visit my folks and, well, what's not to love about my guys? They golf with my dad, watch sports, hang out. My parents know I love Justin and K and as time passes, I think they've come to love them too. They're part of the family now."

Lauren sighed. Everything Lily said made sense, but there was one nagging concern that wouldn't let go. "No one has ever said this is wrong? Weird?"

Lily looked at her for a very long time before answering. "Yes, Lauren. There have been some snide, rude comments, some hurtful remarks. I've learned to ignore them. There are some people in the world who simply cannot accept anything that doesn't fit into their perception of normal. But I love Justin and K, and they love me. When I remember that, the cruel comments sort of lose their sting. Can I ask you a question?"

Lauren waited for the inevitable, nodding slowly.

"How long have you been sleeping with my brother and Sean?"

Lauren looked down at her wineglass. "Since Sunday."

Lily laughed. "Funny. I would've thought the three of you would have given in to your feelings a long time ago."

"Nice to know I've been so good at hiding my feelings." She was starting to feel like an open book to everyone she'd ever met.

Lily smiled kindly. "You're actually better at hiding the vibes than Chad and Sean. It was the way they acted around you tonight that clued me in to the fact the status quo had changed."

Lauren couldn't repress her true anxiety any longer. "I'm studying to be a psychologist. So is Chad. Who'd come to see a doctor of mental health who was living in a committed threesome?"

"I would," Lily said. "I don't want doctors who are perfect. I want doctors who are human."

Lauren blinked quickly as tears filled her eyes. Lily's words flowed through her like salve on an open wound. "Really?"

"Lauren, I told you. My bosses know about my home life, but they also know I'm a good employee and that I know my stuff. When all is said and done, that's the bottom line. Not how many bodies are in my bed at night. Is there anything else stopping you from continuing to explore this relationship?"

Lauren considered the question. She didn't mention Sean's feelings for Chad. She knew that until those emotions were discussed and resolved, there *wasn't* a relationship. But that wasn't her secret to reveal.

Instead, she lied. To Lily and to herself.

"Nothing's holding us back," she replied with a feigned smile. "Absolutely nothing."

God. If only that were true.

"MOTHER FUCKER," Chad yelled. "What the hell is wrong with that goddamn goalie?"

Killian slammed his fist against the arm of his recliner. "Jesus Christ. They need to pull the inept asswipe outta the game."

Sean glanced at Justin, who rose from his seat laughing. "Shit. This isn't going to end well. I'm gonna head outside and check the spark plugs on my truck. It was making a funny noise this afternoon."

"Need any help?" Sean offered.

"Sure. If you don't mind. It's cold as a witch's tit out there."

Sean looked over at Chad and Killian as they cursed the goalie, the coach, the refs and pretty much every resident of New York City. It was a foregone conclusion his wager was lost. "Cold sounds pretty good right about now."

Justin hit the front porch light then rummaged around in the garage for some tools and a flashlight. "Mind holding this so I can see what I'm doing?"

"No problem."

Justin popped the hood and started digging around. Sean had been looking for a way to pull Justin aside since they'd arrived for dinner. While he loved his brother, Sean knew this wasn't a discussion he could have with Killian. Justin was the more liberal-minded of the committed three-some and he hoped Justin could give him some badly needed advice without freaking out over what he was about to reveal.

"Um, listen, Justin, I was hoping to have a chance to talk to you. I've sort of got a problem."

Justin looked up. "Sure thing. What's up?"

"When you and Killian and Lily are in bed—" Sean began.

Justin cut him off. "Jesus. You don't need the sex talk, do you?"

Sean gave him an annoyed smirk. "Very funny. I'm twenty-four years old, asshole. I'm pretty sure I know what goes where."

Justin chuckled at his joke. "Just making sure. Continue."

Sean swallowed heavily, wondering if talking to Justin was such a good idea. He was too much like him. Too impulsive, with a wicked sense of humor. Maybe his advice wouldn't work on a regular guy like Chad. "Have you and Killian ever touched?"

Justin had been loosening a spark plug but paused in mid-twist at the question. He put the tool down as his gaze traveled to Sean's face. "Touched how?"

Sean shrugged. "Intentionally. Sexually."

Justin leaned against the truck and crossed his arms over his chest. "Well, that's a hard question to answer, Sean. I mean, obviously when we're all in bed together, it's inevitable that K and I are gonna bump into each other occasionally."

"Bumping into each other isn't intentional."

Justin nodded. "You're right. It's not. No. We don't touch."

Sean fought the unexpected disappointment that washed through him. He wasn't sure why he'd needed to hear differently. Maybe he was looking for validation. If Justin and Killian touched, than there was no reason why he couldn't touch Chad. Because God help him, he'd never make it through another Sunday without touching him. "Okay," he answered weakly.

Sean was ready to change the subject but Justin didn't seem content to let the conversation die. "You slept with Chad and Lauren, didn't you?"

Sean nodded. He was finding it hard to talk about this—a new experience for him. Usually his life was an open book, especially with his family.

"And you wanted to touch Chad?"

Sean looked away. He couldn't answer that question. He'd never said the words aloud to anyone in his family.

He was bi. He'd known it forever. Usually he preferred women, but that didn't mean he hadn't experimented with other guys. A few kisses, some touches, a couple of quick blowjobs with a gay friend.

"Sean?"

He nodded quickly, hoping Justin would get the message without having to say the actual words.

"I see."

Sean turned to face him. "You've never wanted to touch K? Never?"

Justin shook his head. "No. We're just not wired that way." He quickly raised his hands and imitated Seinfeld, a typical Justin habit. "Not that there's anything wrong with that."

Sean laughed. Justin was an expert at breaking the tension.

"Does Chad know about this?"

"Fuck no," Sean replied.

"Don't you think he should?"

Sean ran a weary hand over his face. He'd spent four sleepless nights since Sunday trying to figure out what he was supposed to do next. "I can't...not again."

Justin stood quiet for a long time. "Not again?"

Sean fell mute, refusing to reveal the ancient secret.

Justin seemed to understand his silence. "Okay. What if you planned a bit of a sneak attack?"

"A what?"

"What if one night, in the middle of," Justin waved his hands around, "doing it, you just sort of snuck in a little kiss or touch or something?"

Sean laughed, long and loud. "I think that's the worst advice anyone's ever given me."

Justin grinned. "Maybe so, but it's the best I've got. You've kinda thrown me for a loop here, man."

Sean put down the flashlight, tucking his hands under his arms for warmth. "Yeah well, unfortunately it's also the *only* advice I've gotten."

"So you're taking it?" Justin asked.

"God help me," Sean sighed. "I think I am."

AS THE COMMERCIAL BREAK BEGAN, Killian relaxed in his recliner. "Tris is gonna gloat over this one for a while."

Chad agreed. "Yep. Asshole got you. Definitely sets him up for bragging rights."

"Since you avoided the bet, I was thinking...what if I just give you my payoff tonight? You could deliver it for me next time you're at the pub."

Chad laughed and shook his head. "No way. Chicken shit. You make the bet, you pay the piper."

Killian gave him a wounded look Chad knew was all show. "We're practically brothers, man. I'd take a bullet for you."

Chad rolled his eyes, though the idea that Killian

considered him a brother made him feel better than he would have imagined. He'd always been jealous of Sean's close relationship with his brothers. Much as Chad adored his sister, he'd always wanted a brother growing up.

As he looked at Killian, Chad realized that was something else Sean had given him—brothers. He certainly considered Sean a brother, and by extension, Killian, Tris and Ewan. Lily had added Justin to the mix.

"Yeah, well, much as I appreciate the sentiment, you're gonna have to save that line of bull for the next sucker. The ass-kicking Tris would give me if I deprived him of his gloating would feel worse than a bullet."

Killian gave him a sullen hmpf, muttering, "You're probably right," before turning back to the TV.

Chad glanced over his shoulder. He could hear Lauren and Lily chatting quietly in the kitchen, and every now and then, their light laughter drifting out. He looked at the front door. Chances were good Justin and Sean would be in soon. It was freaking cold and, busted truck or not, there was no way they'd stay outside much longer.

"Killian," he said.

"Yeah."

Chad ran his hand through his hair. "I was wondering something."

"Yeah," K repeated. "What?"

"When you and Justin and Lily told the family you were an item, what did your pop say?"

Killian looked at him. "You know what he said. You were there."

Chad shook his head. "No, I don't mean what he said right away. I know your pop and I know he pulled you aside at some point to talk to you alone. What did he really say?"

Killian grinned. "He caught me about a week later. J and I were celebrating sweet Thursday at the pub. He pulled me upstairs to the apartment to look at some problem he was having with a kitchen drawer."

"Let me guess, no broken drawer." Chad smiled. When Sean's pop set his mind to speak his peace, he could employ devious means to get his victim alone.

"Course not," Killian confirmed. "We get to the kitchen and he sits me down. Asks me how things are with Lily and J."

Since sleeping with Lauren and Sean, Chad had seriously started thinking about the long-term. One of the main things holding him back was the reaction of their families. His folks and Sean's pop would no doubt take it better than Lauren's parents because they already had one working threesome in the family. Regardless of that fact, he was still nervous about announcing their unconventional relationship to the world. Part of him was hoping Killian would give him some excuse that would give him a justified out.

Killian continued talking. "I told Pop things were great and then he asked me if I was happy. Really happy."

"That's all he cares about, isn't it?" Chad asked, wondering if there was a better man on earth than Patrick Collins.

Killian nodded and smiled. "I told him I was in love with Lily and lucky enough to be able to share the most beautiful woman on earth with my best friend."

"What did he say to that?"

"Said what you just said. The only thing he ever wished for his kids was love and health. Said if I was happy, he was happy."

Chad leaned forward. "And that was it?"

Killian nodded. "That was it."

"That was too easy."

Killian laughed. "It'll be that easy for you three too. You just have to persevere."

"That obvious, eh?"

"The three of you are reeking of sex and cheerfulness tonight. I'm happy for you."

Chad scowled. "You don't wanna sort of punch my lights out? I was a prick when you and Justin hooked up with Lily. I know I was a pain in the ass for a while."

Killian's grin betrayed his words. "Nah, it's just enough for me to sit here and gloat about what comes around, goes around. Sort of makes losing to Tris more tolerable."

Chad laughed. "Glad I could help you out."

Lily and Lauren came out of the kitchen just as Justin and Sean returned from the driveway.

"Get your truck fixed?" Killian asked.

Justin shook his head. "Too fucking cold. My fingers were numb the second I popped the hood. I'll take it in to Jim's shop tomorrow. Let him look at it."

"You guys ready to head home?" Lauren asked.

Chad rose and nodded as Sean turned to grab their jackets from the coat rack by the door. "Yep. Gotta be on the worksite at the crack of dawn tomorrow. Working for these two slave drivers," Sean joked.

Justin slapped Sean on the back and gave him an encouraging look Chad couldn't decipher. "You don't have to be there at dawn. Seven is early enough."

Lauren feigned a shudder. "Seven? Yikes. I thought seven *was* dawn."

They all laughed and said their goodbyes. Sean opened the passenger door for Lauren then climbed in the backseat as Chad started the car.

Chad pulled out onto the street. The ride home was silent and he sensed Lauren and Sean were as lost in their own thoughts as he was. He'd been trying to find some tiny thread to grasp, some reason why a committed threesome couldn't work because, as much as his mind rebelled against the idea, his heart *desperately* wanted it to work.

CHAPTER TEN

Lauren sighed but kept her eyes closed, savoring the morning air. She felt very much like a child on Christmas morning. It was Sunday. While it had been a busy, sometimes stressful week, she'd been impatiently waiting for today.

A body brushed against hers from behind and a strong arm wrapped around her waist.

Sean.

"What are you doing here?" she asked with a smile.

"It's Sunday, and Chad and I were lonely."

She opened her eyes and spotted Chad sitting in a chair by her bed. He held a large plastic shopping bag in his hands and he gave her a wicked grin.

"What's in the bag?" She wanted to be apprehensive, but she knew without a doubt whatever the bag held, it would have her exploding like a fireworks display on the fourth of July.

"Toys." Chad grinned when her eyes widened.

"What sort of toys?"

"The best kind," Sean replied. "Sex toys."

"Oh."

Chad laughed at her nervous reply. "Time to get serious. Last week we only scratched the surface of your submission. Today we thought we might up the intensity a bit."

"If you up the intensity any more, I'm likely to give myself an injury."

Sean chuckled. "We'll take it slow, but sweetheart, we're definitely going higher."

"Take off those pajamas. You're through with clothes for today," Chad said, rising from the chair and approaching the bed.

She sat up and complied, pulling her T-shirt over her head. Sean helped her shed her lounge pants and panties while Chad emptied the contents of the bag on the bed. She tried to repress a shudder at the sight of all the items, but failed. "That was some shopping spree."

"Yep," Sean said. "Turns out Chad and I have a lot of dirty fantasies stored up when it comes to you. Since you insisted on putting a time limit on our ménage, we thought we'd better get busy."

She grinned at Sean. "We could always just negotiate for more time."

Sean seemed more than willing to wheel and deal for added time, but Chad changed the subject. "Get on your hands and knees, Lauren."

His voice was firm and Lauren felt a gush of arousal coat her pussy. She never would have anticipated responding to sexual demands like this, but the cold, hard fact was she loved when Sean and Chad went all Dom on her.

She turned, pointing her ass directly at Chad, wiggling it slightly as a taunt.

Chad laughed and slapped it. "God, you're a tease."

Sean moved in front of her, giving her a quick kiss. "And we love it."

She heard Chad rummaging through the goodies on the bed and she started to turn to see what toy he'd picked, but Sean stopped her. "Nope. Eyes front. In fact..." He reached behind him for something on the nightstand.

She shivered when she spotted the blindfold. "Sean," she whispered, excited by the prospect they were offering.

Sean covered her eyes, tying the scarf tightly enough to block out all her vision. The world went totally dark.

"We're cutting off your senses today, sometimes one or two at a time. For now, it's just your sight. Later, I have a ball gag I'll put in your mouth. Chad has his iPod and at some point, we're plunging you into a world of just music. Today is going to be all about heightening certain senses while taking others away. And we're broadening your sexual experiences along the way."

As Sean spoke the last, she felt Chad's hand on her ass, holding her still. Cold lubrication landed on her anus and she jumped in surprise.

"Shhh," Sean smoothed. He continued to whisper

wonderful, wicked words while Chad slowly worked the cool gel into her ass.

"We're both taking you today," Sean added.

She fought to remain quiet, knowing her silence was expected. The smartass inside was tempted to inform Sean they'd already both taken her, but when he explained just how broad her horizons were about to become, she fell mute.

"I'm going to fuck your ass, while Chad claims that sweet cunt of yours. Then we're switching places. You're ours, Lauren. Today, we're proving to you exactly what that means."

Chad added another finger to the first that was slowly fucking her ass and she quivered. Sean had finger-fucked her there lots of times, but she'd always stopped him from doing more. Today, it seemed she wasn't being offered the option of refusing.

Not that she would. She was already on the verge of an orgasm and the only stimulation they were providing were the two fingers in her ass and Sean's naughty words wreaking havoc on her libido.

"God, yes," she hissed. Chad gripped her hip tighter, her acquiescence clearly pleasing him.

"She's ready," Chad said, and Lauren braced herself, wondering what exactly she was ready for.

Sean moved down the bed, his thighs brushing against hers as he knelt by her hip. He gripped her ass, pulling her cheeks apart.

"What—" she started.

"Shh. We bought a butt plug for you. You'll wear it during breakfast. It'll stretch you for our cocks."

She bit her lower lip to keep from crying out as Chad slowly pushed the toy inside her. It was considerably bigger than Chad's fingers and she forced air into her lungs as the pressure built.

"Breathe out now, Lauren," Sean told her. She released the breath she was holding, the action relaxing her muscles enough that Chad could slide another inch inside.

"It's too big," she said when he pressed harder.

Sean reached under her and roughly pinched her nipple. The pleasure-pain of the unexpected touch sent sparks to her pussy and she pushed her ass up. The action had the desired effect as the rest of the toy slipped inside. She was filled to the hilt and the initial pain of the possession gave way to a pressure that had her pussy muscles clenching hungrily.

"Fuck me," she begged, aware she didn't care who took her so long as someone did.

Chad chuckled. "Told you she'd love it."

Sean ran a comforting hand along her bare back and she knew she wasn't going to like his next words.

"After breakfast."

"Dammit, Sean—" she protested, ready to insist.

He cut her off. "I can always put the ball gag in now, Lauren."

She nearly bit her tongue off in her attempt not to give him the dressing down he deserved.

"Good girl," Chad murmured. "I think that restraint calls for a reward."

Chad pushed two hard fingers into her pussy, curling them to rub the membrane between his fingers and the toy. She started to shove against his hand, anxious for more of the delicious stimulation, but Sean gripped her waist, stilling her movements.

"Take what he gives you, Lauren. No more."

She wanted to scream that she wanted more, but again she managed—just barely—to hold in the complaint.

"Please," she whispered.

She felt a slight movement behind her on the bed, prayed it signaled one of her men was about to take her. She missed her vision, though she could appreciate their reasons for blindfolding her. Without being able to see what was coming, she could only wait, anticipate, the feeling ratcheting her arousal even higher.

Suddenly, she felt something different. Another hand?

"I want to play too." Sean's finger entered her pussy along with Chad's two, the added girth sending a rush of warmth through her.

"God, yes."

They began to move in unison, both of them fucking her together. Their pressing fingers shifted, plunging deeper, taking her faster. She fought to keep from bucking like a bronco beneath them. Over and over they thrust inside her, until she cried out with her orgasm, the pleasure of being doubly filled driving her over a cliff into absolute rapture. How would it feel when it was their cocks instead of a toy and their fingers? The idea sent an aftershock of her climax rumbling through her.

She collapsed facedown on the bed, panting. As her wits returned, she realized they'd removed the blindfold, both men flanking her on the bed, caressing her, kissing her, making her feel like the most precious treasure on earth.

"How about breakfast?" Sean asked.

"I have a feeling I'll need it," Lauren joked. "Gotta keep my strength up."

CHAD PUSHED Lauren onto the bed. They'd had a leisurely breakfast, talking and laughing like it was any other Sunday morning, despite the fact they were all nude and Lauren had a butt plug in her ass. After breakfast they went to the living room, where some hot and heavy petting ensued. He wasn't sure how they'd restrained from having sex at least twenty times in the past three hours, but it seemed as if they all knew how special this time was going to be and none of them wanted to rush it.

Finally, Sean had broken. He'd simply looked at them both and said, "Upstairs."

Chad covered Lauren's body with his, kissing her in the way he'd dreamed of for years. She was everything he'd ever wanted and more. What was surprising was how natural it felt to share these experiences with Sean. Chad tried to imagine doing the same things without his best friend, but he couldn't. While he loved Lauren, he knew those feelings were made a hundred times stronger because he shared them with Sean.

He wasn't sure what to make of that idea, but when Lauren wrapped her legs around his waist and ground her pussy against his groin, every thought in his mind fled.

Sean walked around the bed, climbing onto the opposite side. Chad broke off the embrace, tapping Lauren's thigh to indicate she should scoot into the middle. Claiming his own side, he propped his head on his hand and watched Lauren and Sean kiss. The two of them were beautiful together, years of practice giving them an inside track to what the other liked. That thought didn't bother him as much as he'd thought it would. He was bringing the element of mystery to these encounters and it was increasing the excitement for all of them.

Running his hand along her soft skin, Chad reached between her legs and pressed on the butt plug. Lauren broke away from Sean's kiss with a gasp.

"Ready?" he murmured, as he gripped the edge of the plug and began to pull it out. Lauren groaned—not in pain, but with need—as he pulled the toy out completely.

Sean captured her lips once more, giving her a deep, wet kiss. Chad licked his lips as he watched his friend— and realized it was *Sean's* kiss he was hungry for at that moment, not Lauren's.

Fuck. He pushed the thought aside.

Sean rolled to his back, pulling Lauren on top of him.

His actions went through Chad like a lightning bolt. He was giving Chad her ass, her virginity.

Lauren rose above Sean and guided his cock to her body. Both of them groaned as she sank down on him, taking him completely inside. They'd played for hours, all of them primed and ready to erupt. Sean thrust shallowly a few times before stilling Lauren's motions. Gripping her knees, Sean pulled them higher against his sides, ensuring her ass was open, Chad's for the taking.

"Chad," Sean said.

He didn't need to be asked twice, though as he reached out for the lubrication on the nightstand he noticed his hands were trembling slightly. So much was riding on this act.

They wanted it, and they wanted *her* to want it. And more than just once. He and Sean had talked about how they planned to take Lauren, yesterday when they met up at the sex shop. It was the first time the two of them had mentioned the previous Sunday's occurrences though he knew both of them had thought of nothing else since.

He moved to the bottom of the bed and ran his hand along her skin, wondering if he'd ever felt anything so soft. She was shaking slightly. He gave Sean a concerned look and realized Sean had already noticed. He was holding her tighter, whispering soothing, tender words. As Sean assured Lauren this was going to be amazing, Chad took comfort in the words as well.

He placed the tube of lubrication to her hole and squeezed a generous amount. Slowly he worked it into her tight opening, first with one finger, then two, then three. She was panting, squirming with need by the time he pulled his hand away. Placing his cock at her entrance, he glanced down and watched as Sean nodded, giving him an encouraging smile.

He began to press forward, savoring the sounds of Lauren's mews for more and Sean's groaned, "Yes."

The feeling was one he'd never expected to experience, the moment the most important of his life. Slowly, he entered Lauren's ass and felt, for the first time, like he'd come home. He could feel Sean's cock through the membrane between them. Felt his friend as Sean began to thrust.

Chad remained still for a moment and closed his eyes against the incredible sensations racking his body. Sean moved again and Chad tried to restrain the shudder fighting its way through him. He leaned over Lauren, resting against her back as he sought more of the closeness, more of her warmth.

When he opened his eyes, his gaze was captured by Sean's.

He recognized the look. He'd seen it before.

As he watched, Sean raised his hand from Lauren's neck and cupped Chad's cheek. The caress was shocking, but not unwanted. Before Chad could consider his actions, he bent forward, placing a kiss on Lauren's bare shoulder before moving even lower.

Sean met him halfway, his lips covering Chad's, Sean's strong hand holding him in place for the kiss.

The touch of Sean's tongue against his closed lips jarred him to his senses and he moved away quickly, staggered by the implications of what had just happened. His gaze flew to Lauren's and he realized she'd watched the kiss. She'd seen it.

His heart began to race with fear, confusion, trapped lust. "Lauren," he whispered miserably.

She smiled, the most understanding, loving smile he'd ever seen. "Make love to me, Chad," she said softly. "Make love to *us*."

Her words released the demon in his soul and he began to move. His first reaction had been to pull out, to get out—out of this room and this house, but as he moved, Sean did too. The pressure of their combined fucking was his undoing and he couldn't make himself give up the pleasure. He pushed in again and again until he and Sean were moving in tandem, taking Lauren as if their lives, their futures depended on it.

His climax hit him like an eighteen-wheeler and he felt as if he wouldn't survive the impact. Sean and Lauren followed, the three of them clinging to each other in the aftermath. As they slowly disentangled, Chad fell to the side, Lauren quickly claiming her spot in the middle.

Once again, Chad lay quietly listening as Sean and Lauren slept. This was becoming a habit, his lovers sleeping as he lay awake—freaking out. He was anxious to break it.

Hell, it had already broken. Everything was broken.

Rising quietly, Chad escaped the room. At the doorway, he turned to take one last look at his lovers. He knew there couldn't be any more Sundays for him.

SEAN FOLLOWED Lauren into the living room. They'd awoken a few minutes earlier to find Chad missing from the bed. While he wasn't surprised by Chad's escape, he could see Lauren was upset by it. As they walked into the room, Chad looked at them, weariness written on his face. Had he been down here alone these past few hours, stressing out, worrying about that kiss as they slept?

"We missed you," Lauren said, bending down to kiss Chad. He turned his head at the last minute, her lips brushing his cheek instead, and Sean felt a twinge of anger at noticing Lauren's obvious distress.

"I wasn't tired," Chad lied. Sean could see the dark circles under his friend's eyes that proved the deceit in his words.

Lauren moved to the couch, grasping her knees to her chest in a position that was nothing less than self-protective. Again he was angry at Chad. The kiss had freaked Chad out, but that wasn't Lauren's fault. It was his. He'd been a dumbass and followed Justin's advice. He'd led with his stupid impulsiveness rather than his brain, honestly thinking he could trick Chad into accepting his advances. Shit. Even just thinking about it now left him feeling like the world's biggest fool. You can't trick a heterosexual man into bisexuality. Jesus.

"So," Lauren said hesitantly. "What's next?"

Chad seemed to pale at her question. "Next?"

"Fuck," Sean muttered. He wasn't about to sit in the room and skirt around the problem that was slapping them all in the face. "Say it, Chad. Just say what you're thinking."

"I can't do this anymore."

Chad's words hit Sean harder than a brick, though he'd been expecting them ever since that kiss.

It was Lauren who replied first. "Why?"

"God, Lauren," Chad said, the words sounding like they were costing him a pound in pain for every syllable. "Can't you just let this go?"

"No. God no." Lauren rose, knelt in front of Chad. "Do you think this is wrong, Chad? I mean, I know you've never been very happy with Lily's relationship with Justin and K. Is it the threesome that's bothering you?"

Chad shook his head. "It's not the ménage. I know I wasn't thrilled about Lily's relationship at first. I mean, she's my sister. You know how that is. No guy would ever be good enough and suddenly she's sleeping with two of them. Now, though…" Chad's words drifted away but Sean wanted to hear them, wanted to know where Chad stood. Though he'd embraced sex with Lauren, Sean could see his friend back-pedaling quickly.

"Now?" Sean prompted.

Chad rubbed his eyes wearily. "Now I just don't know. I can't— This isn't the same thing. Fuck, it's not even close to being the same thing Lily shares with Justin and K."

Sean's chest ached as he listened to his friend's words and he knew what was different. Knew why Chad would continue to fight this threesome.

"Tell us how it's different," Lauren said, her words proving she knew exactly what was going on. Sean also knew she wouldn't relent, wouldn't let Chad escape without saying the words.

Unfortunately, Chad's face closed down and Sean knew she'd never get that confession. "I just want to be normal. Live a normal life."

Lauren laughed sadly. "Normal is just a perception, Chad. And those are open to personal opinions. You know that."

He nodded. "There's more at stake here. You know *that.*"

Though his friend whispered the words to Lauren, Sean heard them. Heard them and understood them.

Lauren nodded, and then she looked over at Sean for some support, some answer.

Sean frowned, uncomfortable with her intense scrutiny. He hardened his features, erased every emotion from his face. If Chad didn't want this, he wouldn't force it on him. He needed to find a way to fix what he'd ruined, but the answer wouldn't come to him. In the end, he simply shrugged and looked away.

Lauren turned from him, but not before he saw the pain in her face. "So we chalk this up as a failed experiment without ever saying what went wrong? We just forget it all? Forget what we want and go back to the way things were?"

Chad leaned forward, grasping her hands in his. "I think we have to, Lauren."

Lauren shook her head, fury dripping from her words. "No, we don't."

Chad stood up angrily. "Yes, we do. I never asked to be included in your relationship because regardless of what I might have wanted, I knew it wouldn't work. Think about it. Both of you take off the fucking rose-colored glasses and think about why this won't work."

Sean knew why. He knew Lauren did too. He also knew he loved the two people in this room more than he'd ever loved anyone. There wasn't anything he wouldn't give Chad and Lauren, wasn't anything he wouldn't do for them.

Really? There's nothing you won't do, Sean?

No, he thought. There was one thing he couldn't do. No matter how hard he tried.

He couldn't stop loving Chad.

Lauren absentmindedly buttered her bagel on Saturday morning as her mind whirled over the previous week. Her head was pounding from lack of sleep. She was tired of living in a silent, empty house. Since Sunday, Sean had managed to work eighteen hours a day, every day, coming home in the wee hours of the morning, dropping onto the couch in exhaustion and disappearing again as soon as he rose. When Chad wasn't in classes, he was hunkered down in the basement, working like a demon to finish an apartment she suspected he never planned to live in. She'd found a newspaper lying on a chair in the office with available apartments around Baltimore circled.

Sean stumbled in and poured a cup of coffee. "Mornin'," he grumbled.

She turned, offered him a faint smile. She'd risen early

so she could catch both of her men. She'd hit her limit of patience. The silent routines ended today.

"I'm making a nice dinner for all of us tonight."

Sean took a drink of coffee and she could see the wheels in his brain searching for an excuse. "I have to work the bar tonight at the pub."

"No," she said. "You don't. I called Tris. Told him I'd planned something special. He said he'd cover you. You're officially off duty at three." Tris had been happy to give Sean the time off. It was clear Sean's brother was worried about him. Tris had subtly tried to find out what was happening, but Lauren brushed Sean's sudden sullenness off as a misunderstanding she intended to clear up over dinner.

"Lauren, I can't bail on Tris at the last minute like that. He's got kids."

"And he had no plans for tonight. He said it was no problem. Said you'd covered for him twice this week so he could go to the twins' swimming classes. He said he owed you and he was happy to do this."

Sean was clearly not finished fighting but Lauren's temper snapped. "I'm making dinner tonight and you're coming. I'm tired of eating alone! You don't wanna work things out with Chad, fine, but you better start figuring out a way to fix things with *me*."

Sean sighed. "You're right." He crossed the room and gave her a soft kiss on the cheek. "I've been an asshole this week. I'll come to dinner."

She reached up and placed her hand against his cheek,

hating to see her happy Sean so tired and depressed. She searched her memory, trying to recall ever seeing him like this. He was always so upbeat, positive. The sadness etched on his face was killing her.

A throat clearing at the doorway had both Sean and Lauren turning. She saw Chad fully dressed, his backpack slung over his shoulder. "I'm heading out. Gonna hit the library." They usually carpooled to campus but this week Chad had found lots of reasons for taking his own car. Lauren hadn't seen him outside the classes they were both enrolled in.

"Library? Oh, I could use a bit of time there myself." One down, one to go, Lauren thought. This was the first time both men had been in the same room together since Sunday and the tension was so thick, it was stifling.

"Um, actually, I need to take my own car. I'm checking out a couple apartments near campus today too," he explained.

"What?" she asked. She could see how much his words were hurting Sean, who turned away from them under the pretense of pouring more coffee in the already full cup.

"I've been in the way ever since you guys bought this place. Nothing but a third wheel. I think it's better if I find my own apartment."

"So that's it? That's how you're gonna let this play out?" Her voice betrayed her anger, her pain. Chad was running, giving up without even the slightest fight.

"Lauren, please." Chad's voice was quiet, the sound one of absolute defeat.

She scrambled for something she could say to change his mind. She grasped at the only straw she had left, knowing it was a weak one at best. "You're just gonna run away? We made a deal. Three Sundays."

Chad shrugged. "We only had one more to go. If you two wanna continue the research, go for it. You don't need me. It's not like we were very successful with that whole Dom/sub routine. Too much other shit in the way."

"The deal was all three of us, and we're just exploring, finding our way." She glanced over at Sean, desperately wishing he'd say something, *anything*.

"So I'm breaking the deal," Chad said.

She started to walk over to him but he raised his hand, stopped her.

She paused mid-step. "Dinner tonight."

Chad looked puzzled. "What?"

"I'm making a special dinner tonight and I expect you to be here."

Chad started to shake his head but she wasn't taking no for an answer. "Think of it as your farewell dinner. We've been friends too long to let this end so badly. If friends are all we can be then let's at least start rebuilding that part of the relationship."

Her words seemed to reach him. "Just dinner?" he asked.

"Of course."

Chad shrugged and nodded once. "Fine." He turned and walked out. Lauren fought the instinct to follow him but this wasn't her battle. It was Sean's.

"How long are you pulling this silent routine with him?" she asked.

"Got nothing to say." Sean's short response sent her into orbit.

"We opened fucking Pandora's box, Sean! It's a little late to close the lid. I would think you'd have a hell of a lot to say."

Sean walked past her and headed for the living room. She refused to let another lover walk away from her this morning, so she followed him. Sean dropped down on the couch wearily. "You heard him, Lauren. He wants to move out. We tried. We failed. End of story."

"That's not what I heard. He's confused. He thinks he's a third wheel. You know that's not true. We need to talk about it."

"No, Lauren, we need to leave it alone. You're right. We opened a wound. It's time to stop pouring salt in it. Time to let it heal."

She shook her head. "No. If we let it heal this way, we're gonna end up with a big fat ugly scar. Remaining quiet is a mistake. You two have already let too much time pass without talking. You both need to sit down, say what's in your heart and—"

"Goddamn it!" Sean yelled. "I'm not in the mood for any of your psychoanalysis bullshit. We took a chance and ended up waking something that was better left asleep. It didn't work, so we're moving on!"

"No." She walked over to stand in front of him. "No, we're not. You're not closing your eyes to this anymore,

Sean. You're in love with him. Tell him that. Say it with words."

"The subject is closed." He reached over to the end of the couch for the remote and she sighed. He'd shut down. She'd been with him long enough to know no amount of talking would draw him back out.

"Fine." She sat down on the far end of the couch and tried to put her thoughts into some sort of order that made sense while Sean flipped mindlessly through the channels. They sat in silence for nearly half an hour, Lauren's feelings running the gamut from anger to sadness to confusion.

Finally, Sean's voice broke through the disquieting thoughts. "I'm sorry."

She looked over at him, saw the pain lingering in his eyes, and her heart broke a little. "You don't owe me an apology, Sean."

He closed his eyes for a moment before looking at her once more. "I do. I really do. I didn't let these Sundays play out in my mind before I jumped in. Typical impulsive instincts took over. I thought I could brazen my way through the whole thing—taking everything I wanted without considering your feelings or Chad's."

She scooted closer, wrapped her arms around his neck and pulled him toward her. She kissed him lightly on the lips. "I love your dominant side. Love the way you take control and let me just feel, just experience. I know we've only touched the tip of the iceberg, but I was sort of hoping the three of us could try some more. Tomorrow's Sunday."

"You heard Chad. The Sundays are over."

She closed her eyes, willed away the tears threatening to spill. The stress of the week had been too much and she was so tired.

"I love you," he whispered.

She smiled, blinking against the tears forming on her lashes. "I love you, too."

Sean kissed her again, gently at first, but soon it grew hotter, more passionate. When they broke apart, she looked into his eyes and saw the love and adoration she'd always known, always felt from him.

"I've always loved you. We can make this work, Lauren. I know we can. We're great together. The two of us were made for—"

"The two of us?"

Sean closed his eyes and sighed. "Lauren, I—"

She pressed her fingers against his lips. "Talk to him. Please. That's all I'm asking for. One conversation. No holds barred."

Sean grasped her wrist and pulled her hand away. "I don't know what to say."

"Yes, you do. Tell him how you feel."

He scowled. "How I feel? Brilliant, Lauren. He fucking knows."

"How does he know? Have you said it? Have you told him you love him? Told him you want to be with him?"

"He fucking wants to be as far away from me as possible. I disgust him."

Lauren thought about the kiss Chad and Sean had shared on Sunday. For the briefest of moments, Chad had responded. And, though he'd pulled away, she could see the truth. Even if Sean couldn't. "No, you don't."

He stared at her, refusing to reply.

She smiled sadly. "I never pegged you for a quitter."

His jaw set, his lips pressed firmly closed.

Fine, she thought. She could give anyone a run for their money on stubbornness. "If you give up on this, Sean...things will change. Everything will change. You know that, right?"

He rubbed his eyes and she struggled to swallow over the lump in her throat as she saw the pain, the confusion in his face. "Please just let this go, Lauren."

"You said yourself this would never work without Chad. We've been living a half-life for the past two years. Without Chad, we—"

Sean interrupted her. "We can make it work, Lauren. I know we can."

She rose slowly. Though it killed her to speak the words, she forced them into the open. "I'm sorry, Sean. Looks like tonight will be a farewell dinner in more ways than one."

DINNER WAS A QUIET, awkward affair. Sean had intended to bail, to scarf down a sandwich alone in the living room, but Lauren had different plans. She'd made vegetable lasagna, Chad's favorite dinner, and a pan of homemade chocolate chip cookies, Sean's favorite dessert.

Clearly she was banking on the old "food is the way to a man's heart" saying. He hated to disappoint her, but he wasn't falling for it. Not even a chocolate chip cookie was forcing him into a conversation with Chad. That boat had sailed. Twice.

He shoveled in mouthful after mouthful, his plate nearly empty when she kicked him under the table. He looked up to find her scowling at him.

"Slow down, Sean, or you'll choke." The hidden message in her tone of voice said *she'd* choke him if the lasagna didn't.

Chad kept his head down, his face impassive, and Sean felt his temper spark. Asshole never felt a fucking emotion. Only Chad could sit there, calm as you please, while every nerve in Sean's body was on red alert. His head was pounding, his stomach rumbling. His leg was bouncing a mile a minute under the table, betraying his nervousness.

He scooped up the last bite and put his fork down, the metal clanging louder on the plate than he'd intended. "I'm heading out."

"No," Lauren said.

Sean narrowed his eyes. He was treading a fine line here. While he didn't want to do anything to hurt his relationship with her, he couldn't stay in this room. It was clear Chad wasn't having a problem with bailing on them, so why should he stick around to hash out a bunch of shit that was better left unsaid? "Lauren—"

When she looked at him, he saw the tears in her eyes

and he felt like a world-class shithead. Obviously dinner hadn't just been hard for *him*.

"Please don't leave things like this. You and Chad need to talk. You've been friends too long and you owe it to each other to hear what needs to be said."

Chad looked at him and then at Lauren. "I think this may be one of those instances when time and distance heals, Lauren. Sean and I are fine. We've had disagreements in the past and they always just sort of worked themselves out. This too shall pass."

Lauren nodded. "Is that right? Tell him your topic for the project in Human Sexuality class, Chad."

Chad shot her a dirty look, but she didn't give his friend a chance to refuse. "Tell him."

"It's a stupid project. I told you. I'm Googling the fucking thing, making up a bunch of shit and moving on."

Sean's curiosity was piqued. "What's your topic? You never said."

Chad looked away when he spoke, a sure sign he didn't want to say more. "It's nothing."

"Tell him," Lauren demanded. "Tell him or I will."

"Seriously, man," Sean prodded. "What did you get? Sadomasochism, transvestites, foot fetishes?"

Chad shook his head then his gaze landed on Sean's and held. "Homosexuality."

"Homosexuality?"

Chad laughed mirthlessly. "Gotta love the irony in that, right?"

Sean felt frozen in place, his body and mind numb.

Lauren had set them up good. She was forcing the issue. Refusing to let him escape his feelings. "Irony?" he asked stupidly.

Lauren rose and started to walk out of the room.

"Where are you going?" Sean asked.

"Riley invited me to go to the movies. I'm just a third wheel here." Sean saw Chad wince as she repeated his sentiment from this morning.

"No, you're not," Chad said.

Lauren turned and smiled sadly. "Settle this. Figure it out. Make it right so I can come home. So we can all come home."

SEAN WATCHED HER LEAVE, wondering how everything could have gotten so convoluted and fucked up. As the front door slammed, he looked at Chad.

"She doesn't get it," Chad said. "It's like I said. We're cool. Right?"

Sean stared at him in disbelief.

"Fuck," Chad said, walking toward the living room. Sean could tell his friend wanted to leave, but he knew the look on Lauren's face just before she left was stopping both of them. Neither of them would hurt her by walking out and avoiding this conversation. Sean felt as if he owed it to her to try. Apparently Chad did too. He followed Chad to the living room.

"What the fuck does she expect us to do?" Chad asked. "Shake hands, say all's forgiven?"

Chad clenched his fists and Sean wondered if he'd throw another punch. He was feeling the same need himself, the desire to hurt someone as much as he was hurting. He took a step closer, his move antagonistic. A fight actually might go a lot further than words.

Chad took a step closer too, though his face was still impassive. Sean felt the need to provoke some sort of response from his annoyingly stoic friend.

Sean looked at him, his voice louder than he'd intended. "Can we please stop ignoring the elephant in the corner of the room?"

Chad looked around the room exaggeratedly. "I don't see any elephant." His voice was belligerent, angry, taunting.

"Bullshit!" Sean yelled. "That's fucking bullshit, Chad, and you know it."

Chad's eyes narrowed. "You know what? You're right. We've been living with this monkey on our backs since senior year in high school. Maybe it's time to hash out all the ancient history."

Sean moved closer, until he could feel Chad's hot breath in his face. They were practically nose to nose, each of them daring the other to take the first swing.

"You kissed me," Chad said, his words accusing.

Sean nodded. "You kissed me back."

Chad shook his head, tried to deny it, but his eyes betrayed the truth. "I'm in love with Lauren."

"So am I." Sean watched Chad process his quick

response. "How I feel about her has nothing to do with my feelings for you."

"What are you looking for, Sean? What do you think is going to happen in this little threesome scenario? What's your goal?"

"I want to share Lauren with you and I want to share you with her." Sean took a step away, his anger fading, quickly replaced by the anguish that had dogged his heels all week.

Sean walked to the couch. Sank down onto the cushions. "I fucked up again. You would think after high school I would have gotten the message."

He closed his eyes. It was easier than looking at his best friend since childhood, easier than remembering...

THEY'D STAYED *after to help their PE teacher put away some equipment. By the time they'd returned to the locker room to change out of their shorts and T-shirts and back into their street clothes, they were the only students left. The last bell for the day had rung nearly twenty minutes earlier, but as they both drove to school, catching a bus wasn't an issue.*

They were wrestling around the way guys do. Playful punches, trash talk about who kicked whose ass on the basketball court. Chad had simply reached behind Sean, reached for the jeans that were hanging in his locker. The movement had left them in close proximity, but they were best friends, buds, the personal space between them had shrunk over the years as their friendship had grown.

Sean leaned forward and kissed him on the jaw, just below Chad's lips. Just a quick, brushing glance.

For a second, Chad had been stunned. He'd stood motionless, his face so close Sean could smell the Gatorade he'd drunk on his breath. Sean stood there—his emotions a perfect mixture of hope and fear.

They studied each other for a moment, the briefest of seconds, and then Chad acted on pure instinct.

He raised his fist and punched. Hit him in the face with more force than Sean had ever felt in his life.

Sean's reaction wasn't defensive. He knew that. When he returned the punch, it wasn't delivered as a means of protection. Anger was fueling it. And then all hell broke loose. It had taken two PE teachers to pull them apart. After which, they'd sat in the principal's office waiting for the standard calls home to their parents.

The entire time Sean waited, all he could think about was the kiss. He had kissed Chad. And Chad had hit him.

HE AND CHAD didn't speak to each other for days after the incident. Then, one day, they just started talking. Started hanging out like they always did and life went on. Neither of them ever mentioned the fight again...or the kiss.

Until now.

"Sean..." Chad started, but his voice faltered.

"Forget it. Let's fall back and punt. Do the usual. Just

ignore it and it goes away. If you don't think about it, it doesn't exist, right?"

"You're not gay."

Sean laughed mirthlessly. "Of course I am. Jesus, Chad. All these years you've been my best friend? Look at me. Take off the fucking blinders and *look at me.*"

Chad swallowed heavily. "*I'm* not gay."

Sean leaned forward, rested his elbows on his knees. He held Chad's gaze, refusing to look away. "Are you sure?"

Chad reacted to the question like he'd just been shot. He staggered over to the recliner and sat heavily. Sean expected an instant denial, so Chad's sudden silence surprised him. Was he actually considering the question? Sean's mind drifted to the kiss they'd shared last week. Chad had moved toward *him*—not the other way around. And for the briefest of moments, his lips had been soft, inviting.

"Lauren," Chad whispered.

Sean understood his concern, but he also knew their woman. Knew what was in her heart. "She understands. She's not asking us to choose one or the other. She knows it's better if it's both."

Chad's face crumbled with pain. "I can't..."

Sean rose, walked to the recliner, knelt in front of his best friend. Chad didn't move away, didn't stiffen up. "Can't what?"

"Can't say— Can't be—"

"Why?" Sean asked. It was the one thing he simply couldn't understand.

"I'm not you, Sean. You walk around this world so comfortable with yourself, with who you are. You were raised that way. Raised to believe you could be anything you wanted. My dad won't understand this. Your pop..." Chad paused, as every word he spoke seemed to cause him pain. "I respect him. I don't want him to think—"

"You think Pop would think less of you because of this?" Sean asked.

"Jesus, Sean. I don't know. I don't know how to make any of this fucking work, okay? Homosexuality isn't acceptable to my parents. They're never gonna understand."

Suddenly Sean understood. "You've always known, haven't you?"

Chad looked down, clenching his hands so tightly his knuckles were white. "Known what?"

"You're gay."

Chad shook his head. "I'm in love with Lauren."

Sean chuckled. It was so like Chad to cling to that one lifeline, as if it made everything else go away. "Then you're bi, like me. You knew that when you hit me, didn't you?"

Slowly Chad raised his face, caught his gaze and held it. "I knew it."

"I'm going to kiss you."

Chad didn't move. Didn't blink.

"No more sneak attacks. If you don't want to be kissed, say so now."

The only response Chad made was to lick his lips, his

gaze dropping to Sean's mouth. Sean recognized the invitation—and he leaned forward.

Chad met him halfway.

Their lips touched for only a second before Chad opened his mouth, deepening the kiss. Sean reached up, gripping Chad's face, pulling him closer until he moved forward, his legs clinging to Sean's hips. Sean tightened his fingers in Chad's hair and the kiss continued. Minutes, hours could have passed as they clung to each other. A lifetime of secrets spoken not with words, but with lips and tongues and hands.

Finally they broke apart, both of them gasping for air.

"I'm not the first guy you've kissed." Chad's words weren't a question.

Sean shook his head and he watched as another truth became obvious to his best friend.

"I'm not going to be your first male lover."

Sean had to give him credit. Chad never lowered his eyes, never looked away. He just kept hitting him with truth after truth. "Not my first," Sean whispered, trying not to throw a victorious fist pump into the air.

Chad said he was going to become his lover.

"We're not hiding, Chad. If we take this further, if we become lovers, the world's gonna know. I'm not hiding in a closet anymore."

Chad closed his eyes, shuddered slightly. When he opened them again, Sean was amazed by the difference in Chad's face. It was as if, with acceptance, he'd become younger. Chad leaned closer. "Teach me."

Sean rested his forehead against his best friend's brow, Chad's request taking his breath away. Taking a few seconds to gather his wits, all he could do was grin like a lovesick fool.

Chad chuckled. "Shit. You're not gonna turn into a typical Collins and start gloating, are you?"

Sean laughed. "Maybe a little. After."

They both fell silent, the word *after* hovering in the air around them.

Then Sean's hands moved to the button on Chad's jeans. The two of them worked together to pull the tight denim over his hips, down his legs. When they landed around Chad's ankles, Sean finished stripping them off, tossing them to the side. Chad went commando. Sean did too. It was something they'd always had in common. Sean grinned. Seemed like they had a lot more in common than he'd ever realized.

Sean placed his hand on Chad's face and forced his friend to look at him. He could see Chad was uncomfortable, but the size of his hard-on convinced him the discomfort was based on nerves and fear of the unknown, not disinterest. "I'm gonna suck you off," he said, "but I'm not gonna fuck you. There are three of us in this relationship and I want Lauren to be there the first time we take each other."

He could tell Chad wanted to argue that point, but he suspected that was also based on anxiety. "She won't be disgusted, I swear," Sean said, addressing the concerns written in his friend's eyes.

Chad considered that and then nodded. "You're right. She won't be. Jesus. Our girl is a one in a million."

They grinned and agreed, Chad's smile fading when Sean lowered his head.

"Fuck," he muttered as Sean dragged his tongue along Chad's rigid length, starting at his balls and working his way up to the tip. Sean took his time, making sure Chad understood that there was nowhere on earth he'd rather be right now.

Chad's hands landed on Sean's shoulders, his fingers tightening every time Sean hit a hot spot.

He grinned to himself. Sex with Chad would be amazing, exciting. Watching his friend take Lauren had proven that fact. Chad liked it rough, which suited Sean just fine. He did too.

He took the head of Chad's cock in his mouth and sucked hard. Chad groaned, his fingers gripping his shoulders so strongly, Sean knew he'd have bruises tomorrow. It was part of why Sean liked sex with guys. There was a sensual brutality to it. Guys weren't afraid to use their strength as they searched for pleasure.

Gripping Chad's cock tightly, Sean went to work trying to give him some of that pleasure right now. He moved up and down on his turgid flesh while Chad panted, groaned and begged for more.

"God, Sean. That feels so fucking good. Can you take me deeper?"

Sean moved his hand lower, squeezed Chad's balls as

he thrust down on his cock, not stopping until the head grazed the back of his throat.

"Fuck," Chad said through gritted teeth. "Too. Fucking. Good."

Sean loved reducing his friend's vocabulary to nothing but a few words that expressed just how much he enjoyed what they were doing.

"Can't hold off much longer."

Sean took the statement as a dare. He wasn't about to let Chad come so soon. He pulled his mouth off Chad's cock while firmly encircling the base and applying pressure. "Oh no you don't," he said roughly. "I've waited years to get my mouth on you. You're not gonna let it end this soon."

"Jesus, Sean," Chad said, struggling to catch his breath.

Sean leaned forward, captured his lips in a kiss while he continued to slow the flow of blood to Chad's cock. "Just a little longer," Sean urged between quick, wet kisses.

Chad grasped Sean's hair, pulled his face away. "Make you a bet."

Sean grinned. Chad was speaking to his Collins blood. "What kind of bet?"

"You make me come in under five minutes and I'll switch places. Give you the blowjob of the century."

"You don't play fair."

Chad laughed. "I gotta come, man. My nuts are about to explode."

Sean kissed him quickly. "Deal."

He bent forward and put all his experience into

knocking Chad's balls off. In the end, he didn't need five minutes. Hell, he didn't need three. The thought of Chad sucking his cock drove him to new heights as he caressed his friend's balls, used his teeth to tease Chad's head before taking him to the hilt and swallowing.

Chad exploded in his mouth, Sean drinking down every salty, hot drop. When he raised his head, he smiled as he watched Chad fall back against the recliner, a look of utter contentment on his face.

After a week of anger and stress, Sean decided he'd never seen a more welcome sight. His friend was back. Even better, his friend was now his lover.

When Chad opened his eyes, Sean's grin grew.

"You're gloating," Chad said.

Sean shrugged. "It's just the Collins way. My turn."

CHAPTER TWELVE

L auren returned home shortly after midnight. After the movie, Riley had dragged her to the pub for a beer and some much-needed cheering up. She hadn't told her friend why she was sad and, luckily, Riley hadn't pressed for details. Part of what made her such an awesome friend was that Riley knew when you wanted to talk and when you just needed to forget. Tonight she'd kept Lauren laughing with stories of Bubbles' antics in the restaurant kitchen. Bubbles had a penchant for spandex clothing that was three sizes too small for her quadruple D cup girls, and apparently that wardrobe choice had led to some interesting mishaps. The laughter did the trick and, as Lauren entered the house, for the first time in a week she felt hopeful.

Mainly because both Sean's and Chad's vehicles were still in the driveway.

That feeling quickly turned to shock when she walked into the living room. She'd expected to find Sean sacked out on the couch—his bed for the past three weeks—watching TV.

What she *didn't* expect to find was Sean and Chad sound asleep in each other's arms. Naked.

Her gasp roused Chad, who looked at her warily.

"Wow," she whispered. "When you guys make up, you really make up."

Chad laughed silently at her joke but his sudden shaking woke Sean.

"What are you laughing at?" Sean asked, not noticing her in the doorway yet. His eyes were drinking in Chad's face and Lauren couldn't contain her smile. She'd never seen such utter happiness.

Chad pointed to her. "Lauren's home."

Sean looked over, spotting her. His smile filled his whole face. "Why are you all the way over there?" He gestured for her to come closer. As she crossed the room, her body burst into full-flame. Looking at the two of her sexy guys, naked and happy, was the greatest aphrodisiac in the world. She dropped down on the floor in front of the couch, right by their heads. Sean wrapped his free arm around her shoulders, pulling her closer.

The kiss he gave her proved just how happy he was. His lips devoured hers, his tongue thrusting into her mouth, conquering and claiming every part of it as his own.

"What time is it?" Sean asked when they pulled apart.

"A little after midnight."

She sucked in a sharp breath as Chad's and Sean's gazes darkened, turned hungry.

"What?" she asked.

"It's Sunday," Chad replied. "You're ours."

Lauren leaned back, tried to assimilate to the changes overwhelming her. Unfortunately, the only thing permeating her scattered wits was how badly she wanted to have sex. Lots of sex.

"Take off your clothes," Sean commanded. "You know you're not supposed to cover yourself on Sunday."

The fact that she'd spent the last two Sundays naked in their presence didn't make it any easier for her to take her clothes off now. Things had changed and though they'd all been together numerous times before, this time was different. And she knew it.

Clearly she hadn't masked her feelings. Chad and Sean sat up on the couch.

"Lauren," Chad prodded, pointing to her blouse.

"Wait," Sean said. "Maybe we should talk about this for a minute."

The look Chad gave Sean was one of utter shock and Lauren couldn't restrain her laughter.

"*You* wanna talk about things?" Chad asked, and Lauren realized just how much had changed.

Sean gave them a sheepish grin and shook his head. "Damn. It was bound to happen. Years of living with psych majors. I've been irreparably damaged. Probably gonna have to start talking about my feelings about taking out the garbage now."

They all laughed, but she was grateful to Sean for the invitation to speak her mind and she didn't want to let the chance slip away. "You still want me?"

"Christ," Chad said loudly. "Did you really just ask that?"

She gestured toward their naked states. "Well, it's obvious things have sort of progressed to another level. I wondered if—"

Sean reached for her, pulling her onto his lap. "Nothing's changed between you and me, Lauren."

"Or you and me," Chad added, sliding her from Sean's lap to his.

"So you two..." She waved her arms around, trying to find a way to word her question.

"We haven't fucked," Sean replied. "We were waiting for you. There are three of us in this relationship now."

"You waited for me?" Tears sprung to her eyes and she realized some of her reticence was based on the fact she thought they might move on without her.

Sean laughed, brushing a tear from her cheek. "Guess it wasn't so weird that I was pissed about missing your first kiss with Chad after all."

She shrugged, though she agreed. "Yeah, well, I'm pretty sure I missed a few firsts tonight between you guys, if not the big one."

Chad placed a kiss on her cheek and whispered in her ear, "I sucked my first cock tonight."

She turned and kissed Chad lightly. "What did you think?"

"It's fucking hot."

She giggled as Sean rose from the couch. "So have we talked enough? I think it's safe to say we all wanna fuck each other."

Lauren nodded, accepting the hand he offered to help her up. "That seems a fair assessment. Right, Chad?"

"Race you both to the bedroom," Chad replied, as he took off for the stairs. Sean and Lauren laughed until Lauren shoved Sean on the couch to gain a head start.

They were breathless by the time they reached the bedroom. When Chad reached for her, kissing her as if his life depended on it, Lauren decided breathing was overrated.

Sean sat on the edge of the bed, watching as Chad unbuttoned her blouse, pulling the silky material off. Tackling her jeans as their tongues continued to tangle, Lauren wondered if there could be anything hotter than kissing one lover while another simply watched.

Once she was naked, Chad stepped away. When Lauren looked at Sean, she realized that somewhere along the line he'd acquired some scarves. "The lessons aren't over," he said, his voice taking on the tone she'd grown accustomed to hearing on Sundays.

"Lay on the bed, Lauren," Chad directed. "On your back. And put your hands above your head."

She took a deep breath and obeyed. She knew both men enjoyed her submission. Though they'd only scratched the surface, her pussy grew wet as she envisioned the years ahead of them. Through her research, she'd discovered a whole array of things she wanted to try—bondage, floggers, nipple rings, wax play.

Sean crawled over her, tying her hands to the headboard while his cock tickled her chin. She moved her head, trying to capture the erect flesh, but he kept moving away every time she got close.

Once she was bound to the bed, he hovered over her chest, looking down at her. "Say please," he said. "Beg to suck my cock."

"Please, Sean," she whispered, licking her lips. She started to squeeze her legs together, desperate for stimulation, but Chad climbed on the bed as well, positioning himself between her knees.

He lightly slapped her inner thigh. "Bad girl," Chad said. "You only get what we give you, you know that." He struck her other thigh and Lauren tried to thrust her hips higher, seeking something, anything to fill her.

Sean ran his hand along her face. "What do you want, Lauren?"

"I want to suck your cock and I want to come. So bad."

As she spoke, Chad's fingers moved, the tip of one toying with her ass.

She gasped. Her response prompted Sean to turn to see what had elicited that sound.

"Oh hell yeah," she heard Sean say as Chad lifted her leg, holding it up as he pressed two fingers into her pussy, the action surprising her since Sean's body was a direct barrier, preventing her from seeing anything that was happening below her waist. She moaned as he moved the fingers deeper.

"No," she cried when he pulled them out.

Sean turned, his gaze narrowed. "Tsk, tsk, tsk. You're forgetting who this body belongs to, Lauren. Chad can play with your pussy or not. It belongs to him. You belong to us."

"I need more," she said softly.

"We know what you need," Sean said. He lifted his hips slightly, bending forward to place his cock at her lips. She opened her mouth willingly, hungry for what he was offering. As Sean pushed into her mouth, Chad's finger mimicked the motions, slowly delving into her ass.

Soon both men were buried to the hilt, Sean's cock brushing the back of her throat as Chad buried his finger in her hole. When Sean moved, so did Chad. Dual movements, dual possessions.

Lauren was being claimed in a very dark, very primal way, and she loved it. More arousal rushed to her pussy. Chad bent down to taste it and his tongue pushed deep inside her cunt. Her body trembled, as she was unable to control her physical impulses. She sucked Sean's cock harder and he responded in turn, sensing her hunger. He gripped her head, holding her still, and he moved faster, deeper.

"You're mine," he murmured, the words sounding

almost like a sensual threat. Her gaze rose to meet his and she watched his face as he fucked her mouth.

"Ours," Chad corrected. He added more fuel to the fire raging out of control inside her. He shoved two fingers roughly into her ass as he fucked her pussy with his mouth. His teeth nipped at her clit then his tongue thrust inside her aching flesh.

She flew apart in an instant, the climax catching her unaware. Sean followed, stilling his movements as jet after jet of cum splashed down her throat.

She felt Sean tugging on the scarves, releasing her from her bondage. A part of her wanted to reject the freedom, until Sean moved aside and Chad climbed on top. Before she could speak a word, he was inside her, thrusting hard, fast, his actions proving he hadn't been unmoved by their play.

She'd expected him to race to his own pleasurable end, so she was surprised when he suddenly stopped moving.

"Sean," Chad said.

Lauren blinked rapidly, her vision hazy from the strength of her orgasm. She tried to force herself to focus on the world around her...and it was then she realized Sean had moved behind Chad.

"WAIT FOR ME," Sean said. Chad glanced over his shoulder and noticed the tube of lubrication in Sean's hand. He sucked in a deep breath that never made it to his lungs. Nerves, anticipation, excitement all whirled around inside him until he felt lightheaded.

"Bend over Lauren," Sean directed. Chad recognized Sean was using the same commanding tone he'd adopted with Lauren during their Sunday research. He wanted to think he was immune to it, but the sound had his cock growing even harder.

Lauren trembled beneath him and when he looked down, her face told him she understood how he was feeling. It was her gentle smile and Sean's dominant stance that had him bending over, even though the action was bringing him that much closer to having Sean's cock in his ass.

Jesus. He was seriously doing this. The past week had destroyed every defense he'd ever clung to. Sean and Lauren had dismantled them, brick by brick, until finally he was left here, between them, naked—inside and out. He'd fought for years against a truth that had existed ever since Sean had kissed him in that locker room.

He wanted this. Wanted it with every fiber of his being.

Sean's hand brushed against his ass and he jerked before he could steady himself.

Then Sean's hand turned hard when he slapped Chad's ass.

Shock caused Chad to jerk, the action thrusting him deeper into Lauren's pussy. She moaned. Sean repeated the action on his other ass cheek as Chad struggled to figure out what the fuck was going on. He'd never imagined himself in the role of the submissive, but Sean's rough slaps, his controlling nature, were driving Chad toward an Eden he'd never seen.

"That's what you get for denying us this, Chad." Sean's voice was gruff, laced with anger, regret. "We've lost years."

Lauren placed a soft hand against his cheek and Chad bent closer, desperate for the touch of her lips against his.

He tried to lose himself in her kisses but was hyper-aware of every touch, every move, every breath Sean took.

He lifted his ass slightly higher, careful to keep the head of his cock lodged just inside Lauren's warmth. Silently, he welcomed Sean's spanking. It was no less than he deserved. No less than he wanted. When Sean's hand stilled, stroking his hot, aching skin, Chad shivered. His gaze drifted to the bag of toys sitting on the chair by Lauren's bed.

Sean must've noticed his gaze. He bent over Chad's back and whispered in his ear, his words loud enough for both Lauren and Chad to hear. "Oh yeah. We're going to play with the toys soon. One night I'm going to use the flogger on both of you, tie you together with your cock in her cunt. I'll beat both of you with it until you're screaming for my cock in your asses. The one who comes first will lose...will have to watch as I fuck the other one first. You're both going to learn to control your orgasms for me."

"God, yes," Lauren hissed.

Chad wanted to second her words, but he was too aroused to speak.

"Do you want that, Chad?" Sean asked.

Chad nodded. It was all he had the strength to do. He was barely hanging on by a thread, his cock throbbing, desperate to fuck Lauren, but Sean was holding him immobile with his body.

"Fuck us," Lauren begged. Sean grinned, leaning over Chad to place a quick but thorough kiss on her lips. Then he rose, kneeling behind Chad once more.

"Don't move," Sean ordered. Chad glanced over his shoulder and watched his friend remove the top from the lubrication. He was prepared when the cool lube hit his anus and he managed to remain still, even as Sean slowly but steadily worked the lube in. He wasn't anticipating how thick Sean's finger would feel. Christ, his friend's cock would tear him in two.

Over and over Sean worked in the lube, taking his time as he initiated Chad's ass. The love he felt from Sean's diligent, thorough care was multiplied by the sexy kisses Lauren planted on his lips, his face, his neck. Between the two of them, the temperature in the room seemed to rival that of the sun and Chad felt a drop of perspiration slide down his cheek.

By the time Sean had worked his way up to three fingers, Chad was feeling delirious. He'd begun moving inside Lauren's pussy again. His movements jerky, awkward. Her soft moans told him she didn't mind his lack of finesse.

When Sean pulled his fingers out, Chad stilled, realizing the moment of truth had arrived.

Sean moved behind him and Chad felt his friend's too-large cock poised at the entrance to his ass. He braced himself for the pleasure he knew would be laced with an undeniable pain. Instead, Sean paused, bending down to kiss Chad's back.

"I love you," his friend said.

Chad closed his eyes, trembling as the words washed through his soul like a waterfall on a hot summer's day. "I love you too," Chad replied, his voice hoarse with need.

Chad looked down at Lauren, saw the tears of joy in her eyes and smiled. "I love you both," he said, holding her gaze.

The head of Sean's cock breached his anus and Chad couldn't have spoken again if his life depended on it. Sean's blowjob had proven he was more than adept at loving a man's body. His talent in the bedroom clearly wasn't limited to just women. Sean pushed in firmly, stopping often as Chad's body adjusted to the new experience. Until finally he was buried to the hilt.

For one brief moment, all three of them froze. Chad knew his two lovers were as overwhelmed as he was.

Then they gave way to the most basic need, all of them moving together to achieve the same goal. Sean pounded into his ass in a way Chad thought should be painful, but he couldn't feel anything but the power, the thrill. Sean's actions drove his cock deeper into Lauren than he'd ever imagined possible. Lauren came first, her pussy clenching

Chad's cock so deliciously hard he felt his eyes roll back in his head. He knew he was perilously close to giving in to his own climax, but something stopped him, told him he wanted them all to come together.

Chad lifted Lauren's legs, placed them over his shoulders, his cock hitting different hot spots. Lauren's cries told him he'd made a good call.

Sean's hands gripped Chad's hips more firmly and he knew his friend was also hanging on by a thread.

"Together," Chad managed to say, only finding enough breath for the single word.

It was enough. Sean yelled out as he filled Chad's ass with hot come, Lauren's body shook with the impact of her orgasm, her pussy milking his own red-hot climax.

Sean was the first to fall, withdrawing and crawling up to claim Lauren's left side. As Sean kissed her, Chad took up residence on her right, his arm spanning her waist, his hand resting on Sean's hip. The three of them cuddled together closely, drinking in each other's air and the beauty of the moment.

Lauren stretched and smiled. "Best part about starting at midnight is that we can sleep and when we wake up, it'll still be Sunday."

"About that," Chad started. "The deal's still off."

Lauren and Sean looked at him.

"It is?" Sean asked.

"Yes. I've come to the conclusion I wanna have sex with you two on any given Sunday or Monday..." Chad confessed.

"Or Tuesday," Lauren added with a laugh.

"Don't forget hump day," Sean teased.

"Definitely can't forget hump day." Chad grinned and let sleep claim him easily. He heard Sean and Lauren whispering, his last thought that, for the first time, he was falling asleep first.

Lauren walked into Pat's Irish Pub on Thanksgiving morning with Sean and Chad. The pub was closed for the holiday. Keira told her they'd always held the family celebrations in the pub downstairs rather than the smaller upstairs apartment—a tradition begun by Sunday before she died. Looking around at all the adults and small children milling around the place, Lauren understood the need for more space.

Sky was sitting on the stage, singing Christmas carols with Keira's daughter Caitlyn. His wife Teagan joined in, along with Keira, each of them cradling a baby on their laps. Killian and Justin were wrestling around with Tristan's twins—the young boys laughing loudly.

"There they are," Pop said, coming over to hug each of them warmly. "I was about to send out reinforcements to track you three down."

Lauren laughed. "I had a heck of a time dragging these

two out of that basement. They've been working on the damn thing nonstop this week. They seem determined to finish it." Her words were a bit of an exaggeration. Though Sean had taken the week off to complete what he and Chad were now referring to as their man-cave, they'd actually spent the majority of the week in bed with her. Since Sunday, her life had turned into one long, wonderful sex dream from which she never wanted to wake.

"Finally," Riley said, coming up behind her pop. "I was about to call and give you a piece of my mind, brother dear. It's the holidays. Time for you to stop hogging Lauren." Riley gave both her brother and Chad kisses on the cheek and then she grabbed Lauren's arm, dragging her aside.

Lauren wasn't surprised. She'd turned her cell phone back on after muting it a week ago and discovered nearly thirty calls and texts from her friend. Riley was obviously busting at the seams to find out what the hell was happening.

"Where the hell have you been?" Riley asked once they settled in one of the corner booths. "You don't answer your phone anymore."

Lauren smiled and shrugged nonchalantly. "I've been busy."

"You've been fucking. You stink of it."

Lauren fought the urge to sniff her arm, but refrained when Riley started laughing.

"So let's have it. I need all the nitty-gritty details."

Looking around the room, Lauren spotted Chad and Sean rummaging around behind the bar, each of them helping themselves to a beer. Sean caught her gaze and winked. Then he pointed to his beer bottle to ask if she wanted one. She nodded and turned toward Riley.

"It's a dream come true."

Riley grinned. "So the plan worked. You guys are an official threesome?"

Lauren nodded. "And then some." They'd already decided that they'd announce their relationship—all aspects of their relationship—to Sean's family today. They planned to pull his pop aside later and explain their changed circumstances.

"And then some?" Riley asked.

"Sean and Chad are...well, they want...um... Riley. Sean and Chad don't just sleep with me."

Riley went through the roof. "*What the fuck?* I'll kill them! They're screwing around on you? *Already?* With who?"

Lauren quickly explained lest Riley put her words to action. "With each other."

Riley fell silent and for a moment, Lauren struggled to remember if she'd ever seen her friend at a loss for words.

"*What?*"

"They want me, but they want each other too."

Riley's forehead crinkled. "In a sexual way?"

Lauren giggled, the conversation pushing her to the edge of what little sanity she had left. She loved this family, but she was a nervous wreck about the news they were about to impart. She'd decided Riley would be the best person to practice on. She took a deep breath. "Yes, they're having sex too."

Riley nodded slowly. "Shit. Didn't see that coming. Oh well, the heart wants what the heart wants."

Lauren stared at Riley, dumbfounded.

Riley noticed her silence and appeared startled. "I mean, as long as you're okay with it. You *are* okay with it, right?" Lauren nodded as Riley continued. "You're not squicked out by it or anything?"

"No," Lauren said softly. "Definitely not squicked out."

Riley's eyes narrowed. "You think it's hot, don't you? It turns you on."

Lauren gave her friend a dirty look, hoping to distract her from the flush she felt heating her cheeks. "I'm not discussing this with you."

Riley burst out in a laugh so loud, several of her brothers turned to look at her. "Of course you are. There's no way in hell you can start a conversation like that and then just drop it. I need details. Lots of dirty, sweaty, hot details."

Lauren leaned forward, placing her elbows on the table. "You really want me to tell you how hot it looks when your baby brother puts his cock in—"

"On second thought," Riley said, interrupting her, "maybe the sex part of this conversation is finished."

Lauren grinned smugly. "Yeah, I sort of thought it was too."

"So, it's obvious you've told me about Chad and Sean for a reason. What is it?"

"We're telling your pop today. I wanted to give you a heads-up."

"Cool," Riley said.

"You think he'll be okay with it? Chad and I are sort of nervous about telling him about our new relationship. I mean, while Lily, K and Justin are a threesome and your family is fine with that, I think Chad's a bit concerned about how the abundance of alpha Collins men will feel about the idea of him sleeping with Sean. He's especially worried about your pop's response."

"Have you told Sean your worries?"

Lauren rolled her eyes. "Yes. And we get the typical Sean reply." She deepened her voice and imitated Sean. "My family will be fine with it. It's *your* folks you need to worry about."

Riley laughed. "He's right, you know."

Lauren sighed. "Yeah, I know he is. I guess I'm hoping we don't lose the Collins family, because God knows how *my* family's gonna react and Chad's pretty sure he's going to push his family around the bend with his announcement. It took them years to get used to Lily sleeping with two guys. Chad thinks they'll flip when they find out he's having sex with a woman and a man."

"You'll never lose us, Lauren, especially not me. We're friends. Better yet, now we're family. Sisters." Riley looked over and saw Pop walking toward the food table. "Pop's gonna carve the turkey. Come on. We better grab a seat at the big table."

SEAN CROSSED to the large table Keira had created by bumping together every table in the pub. It seated the eighteen adults present—Pop, Sean and his six siblings and their significant others, as well as Bubbles, and the three older grandchildren. There were two highchairs on each end for the younger ones. The table was loud, bustling with enthusiastic conversations and laughter, and Sean soaked it all in. Thanksgiving was one of his favorite holidays. Hell, any time when his whole family managed to get together was his favorite day.

Tris started passing around the bottle of Crown Royal, everyone taking a tiny nip straight from the bottle. Sean tried to imagine a more wonderful way to spend the holiday.

Pop clinked a spoon against his wineglass and gradually everyone fell silent. "As most of you know, we have a couple of family traditions we like to carry out every Thanksgiving. Tris lost no time in starting the first one, I see. I'll have you know I don't appreciate you passing the bottle the opposite direction from me, son."

Tris apologized for the oversight as everyone laughed.

"Oh, ye're forgiven. The main tradition is the one where we go around the table and each of us says what we're thankful for. I have to confess, when Sunday introduced this idea, it took a helluva lot less time."

Sean reached over and grasped Lauren's hand, placing a quick kiss on her knuckle as the family laughed again. He released it when Chad passed him the bottle and Sean took a drink before handing it to Lauren. He grinned at the face she made after taking the tiniest sip of whiskey he'd ever seen.

"You see, when we first started giving thanks," Pop continued, "it was just the two of us—Sunday and me—sitting together in our tiny apartment on the east side of the city. Then you lot came along and as you all grew up, Sunday's words never changed. I'd like to share them with you today."

Sean watched as Keira wiped away a tear and he tried to swallow down the lump in his throat. His father never failed to share their mother's words with them and it was this tradition that meant the most to Sean.

"Monday's child, Keira, is fair of face, but it's your inner beauty that shines through. Tuesday's child, Teagan, is full of grace, with a voice and a heart sweeter than the angels. Wednesday's child, Tristan, is full of woe that is combated with an overwhelming hope and optimism. Thursday's child, Killian, has far to go, though may he never lose sight of home. Friday's child, Ewan, is loving and giving and smart and kind. Saturday's child, Riley, works—and plays—hard for a living. My word, girl, did your mother have you pegged from the start or what?"

Riley shrugged playfully, though Sean knew she loved her father's words and took them as a compliment.

"And baby Sean," Pop said.

Sean shook his head. Even at twenty-four, his family still considered him the baby. While that fact drove him nuts in high school, it didn't bother him so much anymore.

Pop smiled at him. "The child that's born on the Sabbath day, is bonny and blithe and good and gay, and our fair Sean is all that and more."

Chad snickered at the end and wiggled his eyebrows—the double-meaning of the last word of the poem not lost on either of them.

Pop picked up his glass and raised it. The adults all followed suit. "To Sunday," he said, his voice catching on the word.

"To Sunday," they all repeated and Sean fought his tears, though his sisters were crying freely. His mother had been gone for sixteen years, but they all missed her as if she'd only left yesterday.

"And now," Pop continued, "I'll give my thanks before we start around the table. Oh, and be ready Tris, I'm starting in your direction."

Pop always managed to break up the sadness with a laugh. Sean thought it was the thing he cherished most about his father.

"Being a sentimental soul myself, my thanks has never changed for the past forty-some years either. I'm grateful for the whiskey in me glass and the gal in me bed."

As he spoke, Sean and his brothers raised their drinks and repeated the last line in time with Pop, the rest of the family laughing as they spoke.

The family took turns saying what they were thankful

for, some of the sentiments thoughtful and moving, others hilarious. Two stood out as it got closer and closer to Sean's turn.

Natalie said she was grateful for labor pains. Everyone except Ewan laughed, realizing his wife wasn't joking. Everyone hugged them goodbye quickly as his brother whisked his wife off to the hospital, promising to call the second the doctor declared her close to delivering, so Teagan and Sky could be there for the birth.

Riley announced she was grateful for the seventh grandchild. When her husband Aaron tried to correct her, reminding her Nat's baby would be the sixth, Riley simply rubbed her stomach and repeated her number. While everyone offered the dumbstruck father-to-be congratulations, Sean leaned over to kiss his beloved sister on the cheek.

"I hope your baby is a girl and she's just like you," he whispered.

Riley grinned widely at his words, kissing him on the cheek. "Twenty bucks says you're the only one in the family making *that* wish."

Sean laughed. It wasn't just the Collins *men* who were prone to betting. "You may want to reconsider that bet, Riley. Pop counts as family."

Riley nodded and for a moment, Sean thought he caught a glimpse of a tear in his sister's eye. "Bet's off. Thank you, Sean."

Finally, it was Sean's turn. He looked at Lauren and Chad and announced he was thankful for finding true love

—twice. He kissed Lauren and then, though he knew his actions would shock everyone to the core, he kissed Chad—a full-out, on the lips kiss that couldn't be misinterpreted as anything other than what it was.

The table fell silent for only a moment before Riley and Justin both declared they were the ones who deserved the thanks for the set-up. A mini argument ensued as to who played a bigger role, while the others at the table simply laughed and offered their congrats.

Finally, as the last thank-you was shared, Pop stood to raise his glass once more. "No father could be more proud of his family than I am. Here's to my Wild Irish."

EVER WONDER *how Pop and Sunday met and fell in love? Turn the page to read their love story.*

WILD IRISH CHRISTMAS

This story is dedicated to my family. I couldn't have written about the Collins clan if you hadn't taught me about unconditional love, how to pass the bottle, and the importance of laughter.

CHAPTER 1

"Holy mother of sweet divine Jerusalem," Patrick Collins muttered.

Riley laughed at him. "Oh come on, Pop, it'll be fun. Where's your Christmas spirit?"

Patrick shook his head. "Riley Collins Young, I cannot imagine what possessed you to come up with this harebrained scheme, but I'm fairly certain the spirit of the holidays had nothing to do with it."

"Actually, Pop, I have to disagree," Tris added. He lifted a fifth of Jameson Irish Whiskey. "Spirits had everything to do with it."

Keira grinned. "We're not opening that bottle until later. You guys start taking nips and we'll never get the tree decorated."

Tris gave her a dirty look. "Whiskey might make that chore bearable."

"I said I wasn't fooling with a tree this year," Patrick

argued. "Didn't think it was worth the fuss since we're celebrating Christmas day at Keira's house."

"You need a tree, Pop. Otherwise you'll turn into Scrooge." Teagan kissed him lightly on the cheek.

Patrick put his hands on his hips. "What on earth do your families think of this? You have kids. You should be with *them* on Christmas morning."

Killian raised his hands. "Hey, don't look at me. Lily isn't due for three more months. Justin's looking after her."

Riley laughed. "My sweet little baby Sunday isn't even a year old yet. She doesn't have a clue what tomorrow is. Although Bubbles and I *did* manage to convince Aaron to play Santa this year. I figure the image of Aaron in a white beard riding his motorcycle down Keira's driveway with a sack of presents on his back should ensure Sunday's in therapy for years to come."

Keira kissed Patrick on the cheek. "Don't worry, Pop. We're just delaying the opening of the pressies a bit at my house. I warned my two that they were going to eat Christmas breakfast with their father and wait for me to get home before they start tearing into Santa's deliveries. To make up for it, I let them open a present tonight before I left. Will and I got them the Wii they've been begging for. That should tide them over until I get home tomorrow."

Patrick stepped out of the way as Sean and Ewan huffed upstairs with a large white pine. Teagan grinned at her younger brothers. "Sky and my rugrat are staying with

Natalie tonight. Ewan's hoping it will spark a maternal instinct."

Ewan gave his sister an exasperated look. "I thought that was going to be our little secret?"

"Seems like you've thought of everything." Patrick watched Sean and Ewan carry the tree to its usual spot.

"Just like the trees we had when we were kids," Sean announced, holding it upright while waiting for Riley to put the tree stand in place.

Patrick shook his head in amazement. He'd been feeling a bit lonely lately, but he thought he'd hidden it from his family. Obviously not. His kids were determined to give him a Christmas morning just like they'd celebrated in the good old days. They had every intention of spending Christmas Eve with him in the apartment where they'd grown up.

He couldn't think of a better gift. The dark cloud he'd been living under the past few months lifted. He cleared his throat, trying not to let them see the glaze of tears gathering in his eyes. He had the best damn kids in the whole world.

For the next hour, the apartment was ablaze with light and noise and laughter as they decorated the tree, sharing the memories attached to each ornament—most handmade by them when they were younger.

Tris stealthily snuck the bottle of Jameson to him as they worked. Patrick took a quick nip and handed it back. He happily played along as his sons tried to hide the fact they were drinking from their older sister—who knew perfectly well what they were doing. Patrick caught Keira rolling her eyes at him and he winked.

Once the tree was set up, Sean hit the switch and turned on the colorful flickering lights. Teagan grabbed her guitar and led them in *The Twelve Days of Christmas*. Sean and Ewan cleverly managed to change the lyrics, loudly singing bawdy lines over the real ones. By the ending refrain, they'd all ditched the true words and were singing the most irreverent version of the song ever sung.

Finally, they pulled out the gifts they'd purchased, placing them beneath the tree. Because the family was so large, they'd long ago adopted the tradition of drawing names so everyone didn't go broke trying to buy gifts. Patrick noticed that didn't seem to be the case this year.

"That's quite a lot of presents," he remarked.

Killian plopped down on the couch and lifted his feet, resting them on the coffee table. "Riley's idea again. She said it sucked getting older because her pile of Christmas presents continued to get smaller every year."

"All I said," Riley interjected, sitting next to Killian and lifting her feet next to his, "was I wanted to buy a gift for *all* my brothers and sisters this year and I wanted them to shower me with presents as well."

"And," Tris added, grabbing the bottle of whiskey, "since it's only the eight of us here in the morning, that'll make it easier to watch everyone open their gifts. Fewer people around the tree and no little ones running all over the place, asking to go next."

Patrick claimed his recliner as the rest of his kids

pulled up chairs or grabbed pillows and plopped down on the floor around the tree. "I still can't believe you're all spending the night here."

Keira grinned. "We're here because it's the holidays, Pop. You haven't been yourself the last few months. We worry."

Patrick grasped his oldest daughter's hand. "I'm a tired, old fool. I suppose I lost my way for a bit. Let the daily grind get me down. You crazy kids have reminded me what's important in life with this gesture. It's a lovely gift."

Keira squeezed his hand. "We love you. It's been years since the eight of us were alone together in this apartment...all busy with kids and jobs. We thought it was time we took a night to reconnect. To remember where we came from."

"Oh," Sean added, "and a word to the wise, Pop. Next year, when the girls ask you what you want for Christmas, say a flashy tie or an animal-print Snuggie or some bull like that. Don't say, *I only want you all to be happy and healthy.* Leaves too much room for interpretation—especially from Riley."

Riley picked up a pillow and lobbed it at her younger brother's head. "Way to ruin Keira's sappy speech, smartass."

"Language, Riley," Patrick said, the words a familiar joke more than a true rebuke.

"Sorry, Pop." Her face told him she wasn't sorry at all.

Tris lifted the whiskey, proposing a quick toast. "We're here, Pop, because we're family. To the Collins clan." He took a swig from the bottle and passed it to Teagan, who followed suit with her own cheers.

Patrick wasn't sure what it said about his character that he was proud of the way all seven of his offspring could hold their whiskey.

As the bottle moved from hand to hand, they each offered up words of thanks or wishes for the New Year. When it reached Patrick, he lifted the bottle and proposed a toast he hadn't used since the last Christmas he'd celebrated with his wife, Sunday.

"To Conall Brannagh."

Ewan took the bottle from his father. "Who?"

"Conall Brannagh," Patrick repeated. "If your mother had chosen him over me, none of us would be here tonight."

Sean leaned forward, a definite gleam of interest in his eyes. "So you had some competition for Mom, eh? I never knew that."

Keira grabbed a bag of pretzels. "I didn't either. Was Mom in love with him?"

Teagan looked at Patrick. "I always thought *you* were her first love."

Patrick smiled at his daughter. "I was her *last* love, Teagan. That's a much better spot to claim. Besides, I don't know if it's fair to say she loved Conall, though he certainly turned the women's heads. What's the word you girls use for handsome men? Dreamy?"

Riley laughed. "Um...yeah, not in this decade. I definitely don't use the word *dreamy* to describe Aaron."

"Then what *would* you say?" Pat asked.

"He's hot. Totally doable."

Killian turned to look at his younger sister and shook his head. "Jesus. How are we related?"

"Dreamy works for me, Pop," Teagan said quickly.

Patrick looked at his kids and silently marveled at how different they were. Somehow, miraculously, their unique qualities meshed perfectly, creating an amazing family.

Ewan, always the steady one, hadn't been distracted by the asides. "So Mom thought this Conall was dreamy?"

"All the girls in Killarney thought Conall was handsome, but he only had eyes for Sunday. Not that I could blame him. Your mother was a beauty, with that long dark hair and those crystal-blue eyes. She caught every man's attention."

"But *you* didn't fall in love with her because of her looks, right?" Keira asked.

"*Och*, Lord no. While Sunday's face was pleasing, it was her heart, so kind and compassionate, that I found attractive. That's what captured me by my hand and—pardon the expression—balls and kept me holding on to her for dear life."

"So what was the story with this Conall guy?" Tris asked.

"Well now, that is a tale." Patrick leaned back and closed his eyes, letting his mind drift to a different place, a different time.

"I was working on my family's sheep farm during the day while tending bar at Scully's Pub every night. I was a young buck of twenty when Sunday, who was just nineteen, moved to Killarney to live with her aunt. Scully hired her to sing in the pub and from the first moment I laid eyes on her, I was lost…"

"PUT the horse back in the stall there, laddie. You've work to do," Scully chastised in his deep, gravelly voice. Patrick scowled at the all-knowing look from his boss.

"Don't know what you're talking about," Patrick mumbled.

Scully chuckled. "You've been sporting a boner in those pants ever since our new singer took the stage. Never seen you so distracted in your work. This pub only makes money if the bartender is serving drinks. Tuck your cock away and start pouring."

Patrick flushed, forcing his gaze from the stage and going back to work. It was hard to argue with Scully when he was right. He'd seen the new girl in town a few times over the past couple of months. They'd just been passing glances, but he hadn't been able to erase her lovely face from his mind. More than a few of his mates had made bawdy comments about her, all of them lusting after Old Lady MacKenna's pretty niece.

He managed to do his job the rest of the night, only sneaking four thousand and twelve glances at the beautiful woman on stage. Her voice enthralled him. She sang sweeter than Joni Mitchell and he was awed by her talent with the guitar. Her dark hair hung in long waves that cascaded over her delicate shoulders. More than once she captured his gaze, making him believe she was singing just to him.

She'd won over the entire crowd by the time she wrapped up the evening with a rousing version of *Whiskey in a Jar* when Scully announced last call. As the regulars stumbled out, headed for home, she approached the bar.

"I'm Sunday MacKenna." She claimed a stool across from him.

"Patrick Collins. How about a drink? You must be thirsty after all that singing."

"I'd love a red ale."

He poured the drink, grateful for his steady hands. He wasn't sure why but his heart was suddenly racing, his palms sweaty. He'd never let a woman get under his skin like this—so fast, so completely. One evening listening to her pretty voice and he was ready to pledge himself to her forever. It was a foolish sentiment, and certainly a new one for him.

"I've seen you around town," she said. "My aunt says you work on your family's farm."

He nodded. "I do."

"And then you tend bar here all night?" she asked.

"Yep. That's me. A regular workaholic."

She took a sip of her ale as Scully came behind the bar. "I'm heading home, Pat. You finish the cleaning and lock up behind you, eh?"

"Sure." Patrick was surprised by his boss' early departure. Scully was always the last one out of the pub each night. He caught Scully's quick wink—the wily man was playing matchmaker, giving him a chance to be alone with Sunday.

Patrick smiled. He'd have to thank his boss tomorrow.

Scully said his good nights to Sunday, complimenting her singing and promising to add more tables to accommodate all the new customers she was bound to bring in.

Once they were alone, Sunday looked at him. Patrick had never been the recipient of such a thorough examination. He stared back, equally as enthralled. He felt as if he was a blind man seeing for the very first time. He wondered if she felt the same connection.

"Why do you work so hard, Patrick Collins?"

No one had ever asked him that before. It was simply expected that he do his chores on the family farm, while Scully proclaimed him a born barman and assumed he worked at the pub because he loved it.

What no one in his family realized was—Patrick had a plan, a dream for his future that didn't include sheep or even Ireland. He took one look into her bonny blue eyes and revealed what—until he'd met Sunday—had been his deepest desire. "I'm saving up enough money to leave Ireland. I want to move to America. Scully has an older brother who lives in Maryland who's hoping to retire soon. He's agreed to hire me as a bartender while letting me gradually buy the business. One day soon, I'm going to get out of Killarney. I'm going to be my own boss in a pub in America."

He hadn't intended to share so much. Most young men he knew dreamed of moving away from this small Irish town, dreaming of a better life somewhere else. Very few of them ever managed to make it more than a mile away from their birth home. They continued to toil all day on the farms while drinking away their wages at the pubs each night. What if Sunday thought he was one of those wishy-washy dreamers?

She smiled. "I think that sounds wonderful."

He studied her face, trying to decide if she was humoring him, but he saw no deceit. Quite the opposite. She appeared impressed.

"You do?"

She nodded. "I suppose everyone dreams of going somewhere else, doing something special with their lives. You've set your goal and you're working hard to achieve it. That's admirable."

Patrick had never received such a compliment. It touched and humbled him. "Thank you." Her kindness encouraged him and he found all his private thoughts flowing out in a rush of words. He described his ideal pub, as well as pictures he'd seen of Baltimore and the Inner Harbor. At one point, Sunday closed her eyes as he spoke and he imagined she was letting him draw a picture of the place in her mind.

Finally, he paused, realizing he'd kept her sitting at the bar for nearly an hour. He picked up a glass and hung it from the rack above his head. "I suppose you have some big dreams as well. I mean, a woman with your singing talent could go far."

She rested her chin on her hand. "I do love singing."

"You're one of the best I've ever heard. You'll be famous one day. Mark my words."

Sunday laughed softly. "Maybe. Maybe not. You and I share a dream, Patrick. I hope to go to America one day too."

"Well, of course you do. I'm not surprised to hear it," he said. "Best place for a truly talented singer to catch a break."

Sunday took one last sip of her ale and glanced at her watch. "I suppose I should head home. My aunt wasn't too keen on me taking this job since it would mean staying out so late."

"If you give me a minute, I'll walk you. Not that Killarney is dangerous, but maybe it would set your aunt's mind at ease."

"Wouldn't that be out of your way?"

He shrugged. "I like walking in the moonlight. Gives a man some quiet time with his thoughts."

"And you have a lot of those?"

"A million," he confessed, enjoying their lighthearted banter.

"I think I'd like to hear a few."

"Well," he said, lifting the end of the bar and walking toward her. "You're in luck. Since I'm escorting you home tonight, you'll be privy to all my silly dreams and schemes." He pulled off his apron and placed it on the bar.

She picked up her guitar case. Patrick took it from her then reached out his free hand.

He struggled to contain his grin when Sunday placed her hand in his, allowing him to hold it during the entire trip to her aunt's house.

"I ESCORTED Sunday home from that pub every night for three months, holding her hand as we shared our thoughts and dreams with each other."

Teagan sighed. "What a romantic story."

"Romantic?" Sean said. "What the hell? Where was the part about the Conall Brannagh guy? You sure you didn't leave something out, Pop? A lot of somethings?"

Patrick chuckled. "Well now, I didn't say that was the end of the story. I was just laying down some background for you, letting you see how your mother and I met."

Riley rolled her eyes. "We've all heard about you meeting her in the pub, taking one look at her and falling head over heels. You've told us that a thousand times before. Get to the good part. Did this Conall shithead try to break you two up? Did you get into a fistfight over Mom? I bet you kicked his ass, didn't you?"

"Oh Riley," Patrick said. "You are so much like your mother. Sunday always loved a good story, lots of drama, action, maybe even a wee scene to make her cry."

Riley raised her hands as if he'd proven her point. "Well, if that's true, then you need to step it up a notch. So far there's been no drama, no action and I haven't sniffled once."

Killian lightly tugged Riley's hair. "Maybe if you'd stop yapping he could get to the good part. So you and Mom were dating when this Conall guy comes on to the scene?"

Patrick shook his head. "Actually, I don't know if you could call it dating. Apart from walking her home after work each night, we didn't see each other or go out. I'd never even tried to steal a kiss from her."

"Really? After three months? Why not?" Tris asked.

Patrick considered his son's question. "I'm not sure. I was very smitten with Sunday, but I wasn't sure of her feelings for me. Much as it pains me to say it, I was terribly inexperienced when it came to relationships and maybe even a bit of a coward. I was afraid to try to kiss her in case she rejected me."

"How could you think she wasn't crazy about you?" Teagan asked. "I've seen pictures of you when you were younger, Pop. You definitely fit the dreamy category."

He nodded, grinning at her compliment. "Well, there's dreamy and then there's Conall Brannagh."

Ewan rubbed his hands together happily. "Something tells me we're about to get to the good part of this story."

CHAPTER 2

"Y̲ou're in fine voice tonight, Sunday."

"Thanks, Pat. Could I have a glass of water? I have a tickle in my throat."

"Sure thing." Patrick poured a glass of cool water and handed it to her across the bar. He'd been trying to work up the courage to ask her out for several weeks, but something had always prevented him from making the request. Tonight, he vowed he'd extend an invitation to the Christmas dance next weekend. "Listen, Sunday, I—"

A loud ruckus near the door of the pub distracted them. They turned to see who had entered.

"Conall," Patrick muttered.

"Conall?" Sunday asked. "Who is he?"

Patrick wasn't sure if it was his imagination or jealousy that suggested Sunday's question was piqued by more than mere curiosity. She was definitely checking out the man who'd been Patrick's nemesis throughout his younger years.

When they were growing up, no matter what Patrick did, Conall found a way to best him—be it in grades, hurling, or by stealing the girls Patrick fancied. Conall's family was the most prosperous in Killarney, owning and operating most of the town's businesses.

"Brannagh," Patrick added begrudgingly.

"Brannagh? As in Brannagh Grocery?"

"And Brannagh Boutique, Brannagh Bakery, Brannagh—"

Sunday laughed. "Okay. I get it. He's the crown prince of Killarney."

Sadly, she'd summed up Conall in one sentence. "Yeah. That would be him."

"Where's he been?"

"He was attending university in Dublin, last I heard. Studying finance. He didn't come home after graduation, so I assumed he'd taken a job in the city rather than return here to run the family's businesses."

"You don't like him?" she asked.

He'd tried to hide the disgust in his voice, but obviously he'd failed. He purposely avoided any gossip surrounding Conall, not giving a shit what he was doing. The man had left town and that suited Patrick just fine.

There wasn't anything outwardly offensive about Conall. Watching him work his way through the pub was a bit like observing a greasy politician as he greeted his constituents—projecting a false friendliness in order to secure votes. Conall reminded Patrick of a shiny red apple that was perfect on the outside, while inside lurked a thick, ugly worm. Unfortunately, he was the only person in town who seemed to sense the man's lack of character.

"Patrick Collins," Conall said jovially as he approached the bar. "Holding court at the pub. I should have known I'd find you here."

Conall's words were clearly meant as an insult. A way to remind Patrick that while Conall had escaped the bonds of their small town, traveling all over the country, Patrick was stuck in the same damn place.

Well, not for long, if I have my way.

Patrick had worked his ass off for nearly four years, ever since leaving school at sixteen. He'd stashed away every penny he had earned. His nest egg had grown quite a bit and he anticipated being able to make his journey across the sea very soon. Lately, he'd been wondering if he could convince Sunday to make the leap with him. He knew she was anxious to leave this small-town life behind as well.

"Brannagh," he said. "It's a small town with precious little to do for recreation. I view my job tending bar as an important one. I lend an ear to the downtrodden and provide a bit of joy and relaxation for the men seeking an escape from their everyday lives...and their wives."

Sunday laughed at Patrick's joke, but Conall didn't appear amused. "Sounds like dreary work to me."

"Not at all."

Conall shrugged. "Well, I suppose *someone* needs to sling the drinks."

Patrick's jaw clenched. Taking a deep breath, he silently counted in his head until he was able to control his temper. "What brings you back to town?"

"The holidays. I'm off to New York at the beginning of the year. I've accepted a job with a large American corporation. My father roomed with the president of the company back in the day. I won't bore you with the details, but let's just say they made an offer I couldn't refuse. Thought I'd take this opportunity to visit the folks because I don't know when I'll manage a trip back to Ireland in the future."

Patrick swallowed hard against his growing anger. It was driven by sheer resentment and he felt like a small man for his bitterness. He'd worked his fingers to the bone for years for the chance that had fallen into Conall's lap. Conall had never expressed an interest in America until Patrick did. They'd had to write an essay about what they wanted to be when they grew up during the first year of their junior cycle. Conall claimed he was going play full-back and win the All-Ireland Senior Hurling Championship.

Patrick had written about his dream to move to America to open his own business. He ached to leave the hard life of farming and small-town existence behind. After they'd shared their essays in class, Conall's new goal had been to live in America. And once again, he'd beaten Patrick to the golden ring.

"Congratulations," Patrick said, the word stinging as he spoke.

"And who is this beautiful lady?" Conall turned to Sunday.

Shit. Patrick recognized that gleam in the man's eyes. He'd seen Patrick talking to her, noticed his interest. Conall's competitive nature had been sparked.

"I'm Sunday MacKenna," she answered. A sudden roaring in Patrick's head prevented him from hearing her tone. Had he mistaken the slight breathlessness in her voice?

Conall took her hand, but rather than shaking it, he lifted it to his lips for a kiss.

One day in town and Conall had already managed to kiss Sunday. A feat Patrick hadn't accomplished in months.

"I need to get back on stage." Sunday smiled at Conall then gave Patrick an odd frown. He must have looked murderous. Conall always brought out the worst in him.

Mercifully, new customers came in, quickly claiming Conall's attention. Patrick slowly sludged through the evening, trying but failing to allow Sunday's beautiful voice to calm him. At the end of the evening, Conall met Sunday as she exited the stage. Patrick tried to hear what they were saying, but he was too far away. Scully yammered in his ear, reading him the riot act for screwing up so many things tonight.

Sunday laughed at something Conall said. Patrick gritted his teeth, the action sending more pressure to his already pounding head.

"Are you listening to a word I'm saying, lad?"

Patrick turned to face his boss. He'd completely blocked out Scully's voice. "Sorry," he muttered.

"*Och.* You need to get your head out of your ass, and soon. Before some slick city boy steals your pretty gal right out from under your nose."

Patrick should have known his too-alert boss would know the problem. "She's not my gal."

Scully threw his hands up in frustration. "She would be if you'd pull your thumb out! Lord knows she's dropped enough hints about her interest in you."

"She has?" Patrick asked.

Scully looked skyward. "Lord, grant me peace and give this idiot a brain." He pierced Patrick with a steely glance. "I've had enough of this foolishness."

Scully stormed away as Sunday and Conall walked over to the bar. "Hey mate. I've offered to walk Sunday home. She told me you usually escort her, but I figured since her aunt's place is on my way, I'd give you a break tonight."

Patrick looked at Sunday's face, trying to determine if she was okay with Conall's invitation. He thought for a moment she looked almost hopeful, but he couldn't be sure.

To hell with it. Patrick was her escort. He wasn't giving that up simply because Conall Asshole Brannagh expected him to step aside.

"Sunday," Patrick started. "I—"

"Hell's bells!"

Patrick turned around at Scully's loud exclamation coming from the storeroom. He hesitated for a moment, afraid Sunday would leave with Conall before he could talk her out of it.

"Sounds like he needs you, Pat," she said.

Patrick rushed to the storeroom and found Scully bent at an odd angle. His boss' back wasn't as strong as it used to be, but that didn't stop him from trying to lift the heavy kegs of beer.

"Damn, lad." Scully winced. "Afraid I twisted it bad this time."

Patrick swallowed heavily before accepting the hand fate had dealt him tonight. "I'll get you home, Scully. Don't worry."

He offered his boss a supportive arm, leading Scully slowly toward a table and helping him into a chair. "Rest there for a minute while I get everything settled for the night."

Sunday and Conall joined them.

"Scully? Are you okay?" Sunday placed a comforting hand on the older man's shoulder.

Scully nodded, but the action obviously caused him pain as he winced again. "*Och.* I'm fine, lass. Just a foolish old man who refuses to accept his limits. Pat will get me home and get me my pills. I'll be right as rain in the mornin', don't you worry about that."

"He was trying to lift a keg," Patrick explained.

Sunday narrowed her eyes. "What on earth were you

thinking, John Scully?" she exclaimed. "Why would you attempt something like that on your own?"

Patrick restrained a grin at seeing Sunday's annoyed face. She had a slow fuse, he'd noticed that right off, but when she blew, she blew hard. She'd eviscerated one of the regulars a couple of weeks ago after the man continued to make risqué remarks to her during her performance. Patrick had headed over to kick the asshole out when Sunday stopped playing and set the man down with a string of words that stung more than a kick to the balls. The drunk had staggered away and shown up the next day, offering the most sincere apology Patrick had ever heard. He'd known then and there she was a force to be reckoned with, and he'd lost even more of his heart to her.

"Now, lass, you wouldn't kick a dog when he's down, would you?" Scully pleaded.

A sly smile replaced Sunday's scowl. "No. I wouldn't. However, I feel fairly certain your wife would be interested in hearing exactly how you injured yourself."

Scully's already pale face faded even more. Patrick fought back his laughter. He suspected the only reason his boss worked such long hours was so he didn't have to go home to his overbearing wife. "Now there's no need for that. It's a mere twinge."

"Promise you won't lift any more kegs on your own?" Sunday asked.

Crafty woman. Patrick smiled at her clever manipulation.

"If I give my word to stop, you won't tell my wife?"

"I won't tell," Sunday assured him.

Scully sighed heavily. "Then you have my promise."

Conall stepped forward and wrapped his arm around Sunday's shoulders, the touch too familiar for Patrick's liking.

"Do you need any help closing down for the night, Pat?" Sunday offered.

Patrick shook his head. "No, I'm almost finished here. You sang really good tonight, Sunday."

Conall tightened his grip. "That she did. I fully intend to come in every night to hear that beautiful voice of yours. You know, Sunday, there's an annual Christmas dance next weekend. Usually I don't bother with such provincial traditions, but with you on my arm, it might actually be fun. What do you say?" Conall asked.

Sunday looked at Patrick. "Well, I hadn't really made plans to go. Are you going, Pat?"

His mouth went dry. What did she expect him to say? He'd wanted to go with her, but his invitation was a bit too late now. One night back in town and Conall was making his life hell once more.

Patrick shrugged, uncertain how to respond. "I was thinking about—"

"We can go out for a fancy dinner beforehand." Conall said, cutting him off. "Make a night of it. I'll pick you up around six and we can take a drive in my Aston Martin."

"You have an Aston Martin?" Sunday asked.

During their nightly treks, Patrick had discovered Sunday's affinity for anything on four wheels. In fact, he'd been impressed by her knowledge of cars. She was also as big a fan of James Bond movies as Patrick was. Conall had just scored a double.

Conall must have sensed his advantage. "Saw it in a Bond movie and knew that was the car for me. Come out with me Saturday and I'll let you drive it."

Sunday didn't answer. Instead she looked at Patrick. "I *would* like to go to the dance."

Patrick studied her face. Had she just accepted Conall's invitation? If so, why was she looking at *him?* He cleared his throat. He wasn't willing to continue losing face in front of Conall. He'd spent too many years of his life playing second fiddle to the man.

He recalled Kathleen Murphy, the clerk at the local drugstore. She'd been dropping hints for weeks that she'd be more than willing to attending the dance with him. So far he'd skillfully dodged her, but now...

"Then I suppose I'll see you there," Patrick said. "I was thinking I might ask Kathleen."

Scully groaned. Patrick suspected it wasn't a moan of pain, but one of annoyance. Apparently he'd screwed up again.

Sunday frowned. "Oh." For a brief moment, Patrick thought she seemed disappointed. She hadn't *wanted* him to ask her, had she? Compared to Conall, what did he have to offer a woman as beautiful and intelligent as Sunday MacKenna? Certainly not an Aston Martin.

Looking at the two of them together, he realized he'd been a fool to think he had a chance. She was made for someone like Conall, someone handsome, wealthy, someone who wasn't living on dreams, but living the dream.

Even so...

"Sunday, I—" Patrick started, trying to find a way out of the mess he'd made.

Sunday didn't give him the chance. Instead, she turned to Conall. "I'd love to go to the dance with you."

Patrick felt his heart crack, but he couldn't think of a way to turn the tide to his favor. He wasn't even sure he should make the attempt. Sunday was one of the most talented singers Patrick had ever heard. A man like Conall had connections. Conall could open doors for her career that Patrick couldn't. Didn't he owe it to her to step aside so she could pursue her dreams?

"Come on, Sunday. I'll get you home." Conall took her hand and led her to the front door.

Patrick watched his nemesis walk out of the pub with the woman who owned his heart—and prayed for the strength to truly let her go.

"OH POP. YOU DIDN'T?" Keira shook her head, obviously exasperated with the turn his story had taken.

"Didn't let her walk out with Conall?" Patrick shrugged. "I'm afraid I did."

Riley rolled her eyes. "Criminy. And here I've spent

my whole life thinking you were the smartest man I've ever known."

Sean looked at his sister, confused. "What the hell did you expect him to do, Riley? It was obvious Mom had her head turned by this rich, good-looking guy."

Tris and Killian nodded in agreement.

Riley threw her hands up. "Can you guys really be that stupid?"

"I agree with Riley," Teagan said. "Isn't it obvious? She was testing Pop."

"Testing him?" Ewan asked. "By accepting a date with the rich dude? Kind of a dumb test."

Keira sighed. "Like father, like sons, apparently. Mom was obviously crazy about Pop, but he wasn't making a move. So—"

"So," Riley interjected, "she forced his hand. And he failed the test."

Patrick nodded, never so proud of his beautiful, intelligent girls as he was at the moment. "I did at that."

"She was trying to make you jealous?" Tris asked.

Patrick grinned. "Yes, she was. And it worked."

Tris shook his head. "I'll never understand why women feel the need to play games all the time. If she wanted to go to the dance with you, why didn't she just ask?"

Keira narrowed her eyes. "How was she supposed to know Pop was interested? I mean, he'd walked her home every night for months and hadn't even tried to kiss her. He'd never asked her out. Obviously she was feeling him out. Trying to figure out where she stood. And believe me,

Pop telling her that he was inviting another woman to the dance was *not* the way."

"I'm afraid your sisters are right, but I'd dug my own grave, so to speak. I asked Kathleen to the dance the next morning and suffered your mother's silent treatment every evening for the next five nights. Conall became a regular at the pub, sitting at the table closest to the stage. Your mother sat with him during her breaks instead of at the bar as she had before. Conall showered her with little gifts, making a point of presenting her with flowers, chocolates and jewelry in front of all the patrons of the pub. In a few short days, the town gossips were all abuzz about their whirlwind romance and everyone was wondering if Conall would invite her to travel to New York with him. Some of the more romantic ladies in town were hoping he would propose to her at the dance."

"Propose?" Teagan became alarmed. "She can't *marry* him. Christ! Who gets married after only a week?"

Killian laughed. "Don't worry, Teagan. I think this story has a happy ending."

Teagan flushed. "Oh. Yeah." She shook her head. "Got carried away there."

"Go on, Pop," Sean encouraged him. "What happened next?"

"And please tell me there's an ass-kicking somewhere in this story," Riley added.

Patrick gave her a noncommittal wink. "I guess you'll have to wait to find out. Pass that bottle back around, son." He gestured to Tris. "All this story-telling is leaving me parched." He chuckled as Tris, Teagan, Sean and Keira all took sips as the bottle made its way back to him. The fruit certainly didn't fall far from his tree.

"So the night before the dance, Conall didn't show up at the pub..."

***

"WHERE'S YOUR BOYFRIEND?" Patrick asked Sunday when she approached the bar. She'd asked him for a glass of water—her first words to him in days. He'd been grateful to hear her voice. Then he'd blown it with his hostile question.

"He had to attend a family dinner. He wanted me to go with him, but I didn't feel right canceling at the last minute. I know Scully is enjoying the increased business with so many relatives and friends in town for the holidays. Why does it matter to *you?*"

He pasted on an impassive face. "It doesn't. Just surprised one of you could be in a room without the other. Started to suspect you'd become permanently attached at the hip."

Sunday narrowed her eyes. "If you have something to say about my relationship with Conall, Patrick Collins, then say it. Otherwise, I'll thank you to keep your nose out of *my* business."

Patrick felt his temper snap. He'd been feeling like shit for days, trying to be the bigger man, stepping aside because he believed Conall could offer her a better life.

That didn't mean he was a robot. It didn't mean he wanted her throwing her fancy presents and newfound happiness in his face every minute of the day. "I think the two of you are moving too fast."

Every night when he closed his eyes, he imagined Conall kissing Sunday, wrapping his arms around her. The vision drove Patrick to madness until he gave up hope of sleeping. He hadn't managed more than a few hours of rest a night. He was tired as shit and cranky as hell.

"I don't know about that. I seem to recall you telling me on one of our late-night walks that you believed in love at first sight. Have you changed your mind?"

He hadn't. He'd loved her from the moment he'd laid eyes on her. However, her question sent a barb straight to his heart. "Are you saying you're in love with Conall?"

She didn't reply. Instead she countered with a question of her own. "So how long have you been seeing Kathleen Murphy? I had no idea the two of you were an item."

Patrick considered her question and the heated tone behind it. "I don't remember saying we were dating. Just said I was asking her to the dance."

"Why?"

He tilted his head, confused. "Why what?"

"Why are you taking her to the dance?"

He licked his lips nervously, his mind racing to find a reason. He'd let his pride get the better of him, as it always did whenever Conall was around. "She's a pretty enough little thing. We've known each other forever. Her family owns the farm next to mine. Why shouldn't I ask her out?"

Sunday fell silent and he thought he detected the slightest trace of hurt in her eyes. "You think she's pretty?"

He nodded slowly before the truth fell from his lips. "She doesn't hold a candle to you."

Sunday smiled, though it didn't quite reach her eyes. "Conall's father has some connections in New York. He knows some bigwigs in the music business."

Patrick swallowed heavily. "Is that right?"

"Conall's been dropping hints that he'd like me to go with him to New York. Do you think I should consider it? The two of you have been friends forever, right?"

Calling them friends was a definite stretch. "I've *known him* since we were kids. So would you travel with him as a friend...or as more?"

Sunday shrugged. "He's let me know he's interested in me romantically. I'm sure if I agreed to go it would be with the understanding that we're a couple. What do you think of him?"

Patrick looked at her and considered all his reasons for stepping aside. "He's quite well off. You'll never want for anything if you eventually marry him. A woman like you deserves pretty things, a nice home, the security a man like him can provide."

She nodded. "My own home would be nice."

He cleared his throat and forced himself to continue. "And he's educated, got a college degree and everything. Chances are good he'll go far with that new career of his."

"It does sound like a promising job."

"And it's in New York," he added. "You've dreamed of

moving to America. Conall could take you there right away."

She toyed with the condensation on her water glass. "I've heard a lot about the city. I'd like to see it."

Patrick picked up a rag and absentmindedly wiped at a nonexistent stain on the counter. Now that he'd begun, he found all the excuses he'd thought of throughout the past week falling from his lips. "Of course, you'd be able to pursue your music."

She continued to look at her glass. Patrick wished she'd look at *him*, give him some glimpse of her thoughts. "Yes, there is my music to consider."

She was starting to sound like a parrot, repeating everything he said. It was frustrating. "He can give you a lot, Sunday. You deserve the world on a silver platter." He wished he could offer her just that. Instead, he faced a lifetime of hard work, possibly struggling to make ends meet. How could he ask her to follow him into an uncertain future when Conall's tomorrows looked so bright, so easy?

Her gaze finally captured his. For several moments, she simply looked at him. "What do you *think* of him, Pat?"

She was pushing him into a corner, forcing him to make a hard decision. Did he lie about his opinion of Conall's character or tell her what he really thought of the man?

He'd watched Conall with Sunday this past week. Patrick was hard-pressed to find fault with the man's treatment of her. He'd been courteous and attentive, a gentleman in every sense of the word. Patrick had tried to fool himself into believing that Conall's interest in Sunday was based merely on some stupid youthful competitiveness. After watching them all week, Patrick had to admit he no longer believed that was true. Conall genuinely wanted her.

And why not?

She was everything Patrick had ever dreamed of. It only stood to reason Conall would see the same things.

Patrick held her gaze, and then spoke the hardest words he'd ever uttered in his life. "I think he'll treat you good, Sunday."

She didn't respond, her expression wooden.

Then her temper snapped.

"I didn't *ask* how he would treat me, Patrick! I asked what you thought of him. So far, you've managed to give me a grocery list of everything in the world except the answer to that question. So I'll let you off the hook. But let me leave you with my own list of things that I'd like *you* to consider. First of all, you apparently don't know anything about my dreams. You've assumed that I want to go to America to pursue music. Have I ever said that to you?"

She *hadn't* said it. Not once.

"I want to go to America and I want a home of my own. I want to continue playing my songs, not to earn money but for the sheer enjoyment of it. I want to marry a good man and have a big family. I want love and laughter and a husband who looks at me with love in his eyes, not because he thinks I'm beautiful or would make a nice trophy for his wall, but because he thinks I'm special—and I *thought* that man was you."

Her voice broke slightly and Patrick realized the depth of this stupidity. He'd made a terrible mistake. "Sunday, please—"

She rose from the stool. "No, I've listened to everything you had to say, Pat. Walked home with you hand in hand for months as you shared your beautiful dreams with me. You let me see what was in your soul and I thought you saw what was in mine. Apparently I wasn't speaking clearly enough or maybe you didn't believe what I was saying. Either way, it doesn't matter now."

A tear slid down her cheek. Patrick felt that drop like the slice of a knife against his skin.

She walked away, gathering her guitar and leaving the bar before he could force himself to move.

"YOU LET HER WALK OUT?" Tris asked incredulously.

Patrick nodded. "I'm ashamed to say I did." He glanced over and saw Teagan surreptitiously wiping her eyes.

Apparently Ewan noticed as well. "You okay, sis?" He wrapped his arm around Teagan's shoulders as she grinned in embarrassment.

"I know I'm being a sap, but this is such a sad story."

"Ah lass. I was a foolish young man. Before your

mother, I'd never been in love. It was hard for me to imagine being worthy of such an incredible woman. I made far too many mistakes."

"Oh Pop." Kiera leaned forward, taking his hand in hers. "I love this story. Love hearing that you're human, that you made mistakes along the way. Makes me feel a bit better about the stupid things I've done in my relationship with Will."

"God knows I've done my fair share of asinine things with Lauren and Chad." Sean grabbed the bag of chips from the coffee table. He glanced at Riley, who smirked.

"Don't look at me," Riley said. "I've never screwed up with Aaron."

Everyone laughed, Riley included. Then she conceded. "Fair enough. I've messed up plenty. But this story isn't about me. It's about Pop and Mom and Conall. I swear to God, Pop, if you don't punch this guy in the face at some point, I'm returning your Christmas gift."

"Very well," Patrick said, rubbing his hands together. "It's time for the good part of the story."

CHAPTER 3

"Go ask her to dance, Patty."

Patrick looked at Kathleen, confused. "What?"

"You haven't taken your eyes off Sunday MacKenna all night. Go ask the lass for a dance."

He flushed, guilt suffusing him. He'd invited Kathleen to the dance then proceeded to sit by the wall, glowering at Conall. "I'm sorry, Kathleen. I've been a poor companion tonight."

Kathleen laughed easily and Patrick wondered why he'd never felt the same spark for her that he experienced whenever Sunday was around. Kathleen was pretty and kind. She had a good heart and she was quick to laugh. She was also devoted to Killarney and Ireland. Patrick knew she'd never be happy anywhere else.

"I've been an ass."

"I wouldn't say that. Actually, the word I was thinking

of was *fool*. You're clearly in love with the woman. It doesn't take a genius to see she feels the same way for you. So tell me, then, why she's here with Conall Brannagh?"

"I handled things badly with her, Kathleen."

"You've a silver tongue in that head of yours, Patty. Something tells me you can make this right. Go talk to her."

Patrick appreciated Kathleen's encouragement, but he didn't share her optimism. As he watched her slow dance with Conall, desolation coursed through his body.

Kathleen shook her head. "I never thought I'd see the day."

Patrick looked at her, curious at her proclamation. "What day?"

"The day you gave up. Patrick Collins, there's never been a day in your life you didn't scrape and scratch and fight for what you believed in, what you wanted. You've worked yourself near to exhaustion to save money for your future. You studied harder than most of the lads in school because you knew you'd need that knowledge to succeed in business. Are you in love with Sunday MacKenna?"

He nodded. "So much."

"Will you make her a good husband? Care for her?"

He ran his hand through his hair. "I'd give her anything, everything. But Conall can give her more."

Kathleen rolled her eyes. "*Och*. Damn, you've got a thick skull. Did you ever consider that Sunday doesn't want more? That you're enough for her?"

Sunday had said as much last night at the pub. It was

that sentiment that had kept him awake, tossing and turning all night. She thought *he* was enough. It was a heady, wonderful feeling.

"So what do I do now, Kath? Lead me to the answer."

Kathleen pointed toward the exit to the dance hall. Patrick's stomach sunk when he watched Conall walk outside with Sunday. "You stop the girl and you tell her how you feel."

"What if it's too late?"

Kathleen shoved him firmly on the back. "You'll never know unless you try. Even if she rejects you, you'll be no worse off than you are now. Look at you. You're a mess. Stay here and you have no chance. Follow her and I figure your odds are better than fifty-fifty."

Patrick grinned. Leave it to Kathleen to put her argument in terms he could understand. Betting was his vice.

He wasn't ready to concede yet. Patrick wasn't going down without a fight. He kissed Kathleen on the cheek, murmured a quick word of thanks then rushed toward the exit. God willing, it wasn't too late to make things right.

***

"DID YOU CATCH HER?" Riley asked.

Killian grinned. "What do *you* think?"

Riley shook her head. "Crap. I'm getting as caught up in this story as Teagan."

"Kathleen was a nice lady," Ewan said.

"She's a lovely lass. Actually, she's family now. She married my cousin Aidan."

Kiera perked up "She's *that* Kathleen?"

Patrick nodded. "Yes, Kiera Kathleen Collins Wallace. You were named after her. If not for her encouragement that night, I'm not sure any of us would be here."

"So maybe it's Kathleen we should be toasting instead of Conall." Sean raised the nearly empty bottle of whiskey in silent tribute.

"That's a nice thought, son. Perhaps we should."

"So what happened when you left the dance, Pop" Tris asked. "Get to the good part."

"When I walked outside, I glanced around, thinking perhaps Conall and Sunday had gone home, but I was wrong..."

PATRICK WAS RELIEVED when he spotted Conall's car still in parked in the crowded lot outside the dance hall. Glancing to the left, he saw Sunday and Conall standing together at the far corner of the large building. They were well away from the crowd just arriving at the dance as well as the couples who'd escaped the stuffy hall for a bit of fresh, cool air.

Patrick pulled his jacket around him more tightly and pondered his next move. Sunday and Conall were deep in conversation. Should he interrupt them? Ask to speak to Sunday privately?

When Conall reached into his pocket and pulled out what looked like plane tickets, Patrick knew it was now or never. His legs began moving before his brain told them too.

He pulled up short when the sound of Sunday's voice drifted to him. He thought he'd heard her say the word *no*. He paused and strained to hear.

"Conall, I'm truly flattered by your invitation, but you must know I can't accept it."

Patrick took a step closer to the building, letting the shadows and a large hedge hide him. Sunday was rejecting Conall?

Conall didn't appear concerned by the refusal. "I know it's sudden, but if you take a few minutes to consider, I'm sure you'll come to your senses. There's nothing I won't be able to give you—the chance to see America, to meet powerful people in the music industry. Maybe somewhere down the road we could consider marriage, a home and kids. We've only had a week together, Sunday. I want more time with you to see where this could lead."

Patrick peered around the hedge, trying to see her face. While he couldn't make out her facial expressions, her body language told him she was tense. Her shoulders were stiff, her posture rigid.

"That sounds wonderful, but it's not what I want."

Conall sighed. "Sunday, you weren't made for a life in Killarney. You're beautiful and charming...you'd thrive in America. I can take you to all the places you've never seen, set you up in style in the best hotels."

"What about my singing job at the pub?"

"Just quit, of course. I have money. I can take care of you."

Sunday shook her head. "I like working."

Conall scoffed. "You can't seriously tell me you like singing night after night in a dingy pub for a bunch of dirty farmers."

Conall said *farmers* like he'd just swallowed something nasty. Patrick's temper rose.

"I have no problem with the pub or the patrons there. And I don't mind working, Conall, if it would help my husband and family."

"But that's just it, Sunday. If you come with me, you won't have to get your hands dirty. I'll rent you a big, fancy apartment and even hire a maid for you. I'll be working with a very prestigious firm and I'll need a pretty lady on my arm. We'll throw the biggest parties for the cream of New York society. You'll be the premiere hostess and other women will look to *you* as the one to emulate."

Conall made it sound like the only thing Sunday had going for her was a pretty face and good manners. Patrick took a step closer, ready to call a halt to Conall's insulting proposal, but Sunday's response stopped him again.

"I don't want to give parties, Conall. I sincerely hope to God I have more to offer than rubbing elbows with rich snobs and looking down my nose at people who work hard to make a living. People who don't judge another person's character based solely on how much money they have in the bank."

Her tone was hostile. Even Patrick could hear the venom in each word. Her anger wasn't lost on Conall either.

"Christ. You sound just like Patrick Collins."

Sunday lifted her chin defensively. "I take that as a compliment. Patrick is an honorable, honest, hard-working man."

Conall's eyes narrowed. "Are you in *love* with him?"

Patrick held his breath and leaned closer. Would she admit it? Were her feelings toward him that strong?

Sunday didn't reply, but something in her face must've given her feelings away because Conall's scowl grew.

"You are! You're in love with Patrick Collins. Jesus! I credited you with more intelligence than to fall for that ne'er-do-well. He's a barkeep and a farmer with a bunch of big dreams that will never come true. Why would you tie yourself to a miserable existence with someone like that?"

Patrick clenched his fists.

Apparently he wasn't the only one whose anger had been tweaked.

Sunday exploded. "Patrick Collins is the finest man I've ever met! He's compassionate and kind. How can you stand here and smugly criticize a man who's had to work for everything he's ever earned? You've had the world handed to you on a silver platter. There's nothing *special* about that, Conall."

Conall leaned closer. "Is that what you think? Look what that hard work has earned him. Nothing but calluses and holes in his boots. You deserve more than that, Sunday."

"You aren't fit to *lick* those boots!" Sunday planted her hands on her hips and turned slightly, allowing the street-light to capture her face. Patrick marveled at the intimidating look he saw there. She was a powerhouse. He loved her.

Patrick had heard enough. Hell would freeze over before he let Conall continue to criticize Sunday.

"It's clear you aren't going to listen to reason. Maybe you need another type of persuasion. I bet your farm boy's never even kissed you." Conall grabbed Sunday and took her lips roughly.

Patrick sprang out of his hiding spot as Sunday shoved against Conall's shoulders.

"Stop!" she cried.

Conall wouldn't be deterred. His hand grasped Sunday's breast, squeezing.

Patrick captured Conall's wrist and twisted, hard, forcing the man to release Sunday. He shoved Conall farther away.

It was clear from the shocked look on his enemy's face, Conall hadn't expected to be interrupted. "Oh look," he sneered. "It's the barkeep. Just in time, too. I'm parched. Go fetch me an ale."

Patrick reacted without thought. He punched Conall in the face, following with a solid blow to the gut. Conall dropped like a sack of potatoes.

"How dare you lay a hand on her!" Patrick shouted.

"Didn't you hear her say 'stop'? What's wrong, rich boy? Hasn't anyone ever said *no* to you before?"

Sunday's hand landed on his arm. Patrick stiffened. "Pat. It's okay. I'm fine."

Patrick wasn't soothed. "No, Sunday. It's not."

Conall staggered to his feet and Patrick thought the man was going take a few swings of his own. Patrick had broken up more than his fair share of barroom brawls. He had no doubt he could handle one spoiled college boy.

He gestured for Conall to step closer. "Come on, Conall. I've been waiting a lifetime for this."

Conall paused, his gaze traveling from Patrick to Sunday and back again. "Fuck it," he said at last. "She's not worth it."

Patrick's world went red. "You stupid bastard. You've spent your entire life placing value on the wrong things. Sunday is *priceless*. You're going to realize that one day and you know what?"

"What?" Conall spat belligerently, rubbing his jaw.

"It'll be too late."

Conall studied Patrick's face for a long time. Then he shrugged. "It was too late before it started. Take her, Pat. You two deserve each other." Conall staggered away, his last words meant to be an insult.

Patrick didn't take them as one. He turned to face her. "I'm sorry, Sunday."

She frowned then rolled her eyes. "Sorry? For what part, Pat? The part where you pulled that asshole off me?

Or maybe when you said I was priceless? Is that what you're sorry about?"

He shook his head. "No."

"Did you mean it?"

"Christ, lass. Do you really have to ask? You're a treasure beyond measure, but Conall was right. What can I give you that will show you how much you mean to me?"

"Your heart. Give me your heart, Pat. It'll be more than enough."

He leaned forward and pressed his brow against hers, shutting his eyes tightly. "You have that. You'll always have that. I love you, Sunday."

Sunday reached up and placed her hands on Patrick's face. She waited until he opened his eyes to look at her. "And I love you."

"YES!" Riley stood up and high-fived Sean across the coffee table.

Patrick chuckled at his youngest daughter's exuberant response. "I assume this means you approve of the happy ending?"

"Hell yeah. You punched that coward twice! That was totally cool, Pop." Riley resumed her seat on the couch.

"So whatever happened to Conall Brannagh?" Ewan asked.

"Ah, well, that's a story in itself. He took the fancy job in New York, but he couldn't cut it as a high-powered business executive. He was fired before the end of the first year and returned to Killarney, where he managed to run his family's businesses into bankruptcy in less than a decade. Now he's the barkeep at Scully's."

Teagan's eyes widened. "Really?"

Patrick's grin grew. "No. Not really. Last I heard, he and his third trophy wife were living in Manhattan."

Teagan rolled her eyes. "Nice, Pop. You got me."

They all laughed. The conversation continued into the wee hours until, eventually, everyone began to make their way to bed.

Sean was the last to rise.

"It was a good story, Pop."

Patrick nodded. "I think so too."

"I wish there'd been a happier ending. Mom should have been here tonight."

Patrick swallowed heavily against the lump in his throat. Cancer had claimed Sunday well before her time. For too many years he'd wished the same thing. Eventually, he'd learned to be grateful for the time they'd had together. "She was here, Sean. She's always been here. She's inside you and your brothers and sisters. She's in at least fifty percent of those Christmas ornaments, in dozens of the pictures, and she's in quite a bit of the furniture around here. We had a heck of a fight the day I dragged that ugly old recliner in here. I think of her every time I sit down. She created this home for all of us."

"It's not the same thing. You know what I mean, Pop."

"You didn't listen to the story. Your mother achieved

every one of her goals—she got her home, her family, her life in America. She told me the night before she passed away she was a woman dying without a single regret. She said she'd lived a full life with love and laughter and she couldn't ask for more. I suppose that's the best any of us can wish for, son."

Sean put his hands in the pockets of his jeans then gave him a crooked grin. "You're right. I hope I can say the same thing when I die."

"I hope we all can."

CHAPTER 4

P atrick listened to the hushed voices coming from the bedrooms. The girls were giggling in their room. Tris and Killian's deep tones drifted down the stairs. Ewan and Sean were teasing each other, and for a moment, he thought he'd have to break up what sounded like a wrestling match.

He closed his eyes and recalled the last part of the story. The one he hadn't told his children.

PATRICK WONDERED if he'd ever lived a more perfect moment as he and Sunday held hands, walking through the quiet streets of town toward her home. The neighbors who weren't still celebrating the holidays at the dance were snuggled in warm beds in dark houses. It felt as if they were the only two people on the planet.

They walked in silence as Patrick tried to wrap his head around what had just taken place. Sunday had turned Conall down for *him*. She'd told him she loved him.

Sunday paused when they reached the door of her aunt's home. "My aunt isn't home."

Patrick was surprised by Sunday's quiet admission. "She's not?"

Sunday shook her head almost shyly. "She's spending the night at her brother's house. She's doing Christmas morning with my Uncle Ryan and his family. I'm going to join them for dinner tomorrow."

"Oh."

Sunday glanced over her shoulder at the empty house and bit her lip. "Do you want to come in?"

Suddenly her reticence made sense. His heart raced. "I'd like to. Very much."

She smiled, opening the door. Patrick crossed the threshold, feeling almost dizzy as he considered what he hoped would happen tonight.

Once they entered, he briefly glanced around her aunt's parlor. Though he'd walked Sunday to the door nearly a hundred times the past few months, he'd never been inside.

Sunday didn't move and her anxiety was almost a tangible being in the darkened house. He stroked her face, savoring the soft skin of her cheek, hoping his touch would calm her. "You're so beautiful," he whispered.

Sunday released a long breath. "I've never..." She didn't finish her thought.

He kissed her brow and wrapped her in his embrace. "Neither have I."

She put her arms around his waist, holding him tightly.

"Sunday. I can leave if you aren't ready for—"

She pressed her lips to his before he could finish speaking and opened them. Patrick accepted her invitation, dipping his tongue into her sweet mouth. She tasted like soda and cookies. He closed his eyes and took more, deepening the kiss.

Sunday's fingers tangled in his hair, pulling him closer, her hungry kisses rivaling his. For several minutes, he let himself disappear into her soft sighs and rough touches.

When they separated, Sunday's gaze met his.

"I love you," he said again. The words had been written on his heart since the first night he saw her. It felt so good, so right to be able to speak them aloud.

"I love you too."

He ran his fingers through her long black hair. "Where's your bedroom?"

Even in the dim lighting, he saw the flush on her face. If she gave the slightest sign of hesitation, he'd leave.

She didn't. Sunday took his hand in hers and led him down the hallway to the last bedroom. She walked to the nightstand and turned on a small lamp. It cast a soft light that illuminated the room enough for him to look around.

She hadn't lived in Killarney long, so Patrick was surprised by how much the small room reflected her. Her battered guitar case was tucked in the corner. The bookshelf was overflowing with paperbacks and notebooks. On the wall, she'd surrounded herself with photographs of family and friends. Sunday valued the people in her life more than anything else. Patrick had lost sight of that fact, lost in his own insecurities. He wouldn't make the same mistake again.

He looked at her bed, rubbing his palms against his pants. He ached with need...and nervousness.

"You've really never done this?" Sunday asked.

He shook his head. "I've never been in love before you, Sunday. You've changed my world."

She lifted his hand, pressing her lips against his knuckles. "You've *become* my world."

After that, their words gave way to motion. Patrick kissed her gently before unbuttoning her blouse. Sunday stood still as he slowly worked each button free. The blouse fell open and Patrick slipped his hands beneath the silky material at her shoulders to push it off.

His breath caught as he looked at her pale breasts covered by a lacy bra. He cupped them, enjoying Sunday's soft murmur of appreciation when he squeezed the sensitive flesh.

Her hands landed on his forearms, not to push him away but to steady herself. She swayed and her eyes closed as if she were mesmerized by his touch. He placed a kiss on her bare shoulder after lifting her bra strap and pulling it down. His lips traveled along her shoulder to her neck, from her neck to her ear.

Sunday's rapid breathing, the rise and fall of her chest,

the pulse at her neck told him she was enjoying his journey as much as he was.

He repeated the motion on the other side then reached behind her to unclasp the bra. Sunday froze as he peeled the lace away. Neither of them moved as Patrick looked at his lovely lady. The image of her standing topless before him was something he'd never forget. He was hers. He belonged to her, and he made a silent promise that as long as he was living, he'd never love another woman the way he loved Sunday.

Bending his head, he took one of her tight nipples in his mouth.

"Ahh!" Sunday cried in shock and pleasure. "God, Pat. That feels amazing."

He sucked harder. Her hands flew to his head, pulling his hair almost painfully.

He played with her breasts until Sunday called out for mercy. Lifting his head, he wasn't surprised to find her face and body flushed. It was hot in the room...so damn hot.

He unbuttoned his shirt, not taking the time or care he'd used while helping her shed hers. The fabric tore in his haste to remove it. Sunday gave him a soft smile, but she didn't attempt to slow him down. Once his shirt lay on the floor by her blouse, Sunday was there, her hands stroking his chest, toying with the light smattering of hair.

Patrick swallowed heavily and prayed for the strength to finish this night with some shred of dignity when Sunday's lips landed on *his* nipple. She lightly bit the tight nub until Patrick felt certain he would explode. He wanted her too badly for this to last long.

He cupped her face in his palms. "Sunday." He fought to find the words, but his face must have said it all. Sunday took a step away from him and, as he held his breath, she pushed her skirt and panties over her hips.

A wave of lightheadedness caused him to sway slightly. She was simply stunning.

"Go lay down on the bed, love."

She moved slowly away from him as Patrick counted to twenty in his head. He was in serious danger of losing control.

Sunday lay in the middle of the mattress then shyly beckoned him to come closer. He took the five steps necessary to reach her side then sat on the edge of the bed, his gaze devouring every tantalizing inch of her body. He caressed her, letting his fingers explore her breasts, her stomach, her thighs.

Silently, he urged her to open her legs. They parted. Patrick took a deep breath. His hand trembled slightly when he reached between them.

Sunday gasped when he ran his finger along her wet nether lips. He leaned forward and kissed her. "We can stop at any point, Sunday."

She shook her head. "Don't you dare."

He chuckled before pressing his lips against hers once more. He found her clit with his fingers, enjoying her intense reaction as he applied pressure.

She turned her head away from his kiss. "Oh my God. Oh my God!"

Her passion sparked his. He became bolder, more confident as he continued his explorations. Sunday's hands flew to his shoulders, squeezing the muscles there tightly when he slowly pushed a finger inside her.

She was tight and hot and—mercifully—so wet. He knew she was as tense as he was, but she wasn't letting that emotion overpower her needs, her desires. Gently, he worked his finger in and out of her passage as her hips rocked to meet him, encouraging him to go deeper, thrust harder.

Patrick added a second finger and pressed her clit with his thumb. Sunday exploded. Her inner muscles clenched against him as she came. Her hands clamped on his arms so hard, he knew she'd leave bruises.

He stilled his movements, kissing her softly as her orgasm ran its course. He whispered sweet nothings until her wits returned.

"Okay?" he asked.

She laughed quietly. "Are you kidding? Do that again."

He grinned. "Mind if I join you this time?"

She shook her head. "Hurry up."

"Damn. Didn't expect you to be such a demanding, greedy lover."

She tilted her head. "Is that going to be a problem?"

"Hell no." Patrick stood. He reached for the button on his pants and Sunday propped herself up on one elbow, her expression equal parts curiosity and apprehension.

"Moment of truth," he muttered.

Sunday's smile grew. "I showed you mine. It's only fair I get to see yours."

Suddenly a lifetime of sleeping with Sunday passed before his eyes and the rightness of the moment solidified. He'd expected their first time to be awkward, uncomfortable. Instead, it was the perfect blend of wonder and laughter.

He pushed his pants down, kicking off his shoes at the same time. His erection was standing at full-mast and he prayed he could keep it that way long enough to get inside her. Sunday licked her lips as she looked at him and Patrick knew his concern was genuine. He'd never make it at this rate.

He was about to join her on the bed when he remembered something. He bent over to retrieve his wallet from his pants.

Sunday watched him questioningly.

"Um, Sunday. I hope you won't take this the wrong way."

She frowned. "What do you mean?"

"I bought condoms a couple of weeks ago."

Sunday sat up. "For me or for Kathleen?"

"Don't be silly, lass. Of course I bought them for you."

"Bit sure of yourself, weren't you?"

He shrugged, pulling a condom out of his wallet and donning it. "I'm not sure it was cockiness so much as hope."

She giggled and lay back down. "Come here and show me some of that cockiness."

"I can see the regulars in the pub haven't been a good influence on you." He climbed onto the bed and crawled over Sunday's body. The humor dispersed at their close proximity. Patrick listened to Sunday's breathing quicken, felt his own heart rate accelerate.

He kissed her softly as he placed the head of his member at her opening. Sunday wrapped her legs around his. Patrick was blown away by her complete faith in him. She trusted him to protect her, to keep her safe.

He'd never let her down. He watched her face carefully, giving her one last chance to change her mind, to call a halt.

Sunday captured his gaze. "Don't stop, Pat."

"Should I do this quickly?"

She nodded.

He retreated a fraction of an inch then returned with a hard press. He broke through the thin restraint, taking her virginity as surely as he gave his own.

Sunday gasped and held him tightly, her grip around his shoulders nearly impenetrable. Patrick froze, buried completely inside her. He forced air into his lungs and fought the urge to come. It took every ounce of strength in his body, but somehow he managed to beat back the need to erupt.

Neither of them moved for several long moments.

Sunday broke the silence first. "Are you okay?"

"I can't move."

She cupped his face and looked at him. "Are you hurt?"

"If I move the slightest bit, I'm going to come, love. I think this is going to be the shortest sex in history."

Sunday laughed, the motion jarring him enough that he groaned and gritted his teeth.

"Dammit. Don't laugh. You're killing me."

Sunday sobered up, but barely. She was still grinning when she spoke. "Come, Pat. We have plenty of time to perfect this. We have forever."

He didn't need to hear more. His body was in agony, demanding release. He pulled out a few inches then slid back in. He managed four good thrusts before he exploded. He wasn't certain, but he thought his eyes rolled back in his head and he was worried he'd overflowed the condom. He'd never felt anything so intense, so fucking incredible.

Patrick held himself on his elbows above her precious body as a stream of words flew from him—a mixture of sweet words of love and dirty promises of how he was going to make this up to her.

Sunday simply stroked his back until his climax subsided and sanity returned.

"Tonight is the best night of my life," she said when he pulled out of her body, rolled to the side and enfolded her in his embrace.

"Mine too. I didn't realize that would be..." Patrick had never had a problem stating how he felt, but with Sunday, he never seemed able to find a powerful enough sentiment.

"I didn't either."

"You didn't even come that last time. God, you must think I'm an ass."

Sunday gave him an exasperated look.

"Give me ten minutes and I swear I'll do better," he added quickly.

"Nothing could be better. I'm so happy you were my first, Pat. And you were wonderful. Better than I could have imagined."

He kissed her softly on the cheek. "Let me go clean up." He quickly dashed to the bathroom to dispose of the condom. He cleaned himself up before grabbing a washcloth and wetting it. He returned to the bedroom and crawled back into bed.

He silently bid Sunday to open her legs and carefully washed her. She blushed with his ministrations, but lay quietly until he finished.

"There's something I've always wondered, but I've never remembered to ask. How did you get your name? Were you born on a Sunday?"

She laughed. "No, though I'm sure everyone thinks so. I was actually born on a Thursday."

Patrick grinned. "I'm guessing there's a story here."

Sunday nodded. "I'm Irish. Of course there is. My mother was in labor for nearly a week before I was born."

Patrick made a pained expression "A week? Ouch."

"Yep. A long, rainy, dreary week. According to my da, it rained cats and dogs for seven whole days as my mother lay in bed suffering from labor pains. When I finally made my much overdue appearance, my da swears the clouds broke and the sun shone through. While he was remarking about the change in the weather, my mother was proclaiming she needed a day of rest. Da said they looked at each other and said *Sunday* at the exact same time. My father loved to spin yarns, so whether or not any of that is true, I can't say. Even so, it's a nice story."

Patrick kissed her on the cheek. "God knows you brought sunshine and peace to my life the day you walked into that bar."

Sunday blinked and Patrick thought he saw the sheen of tears in her eyes. "You are a romantic man, Patrick Collins."

He laughed. "Don't tell anyone. We barmen have a reputation to uphold."

"Ah, yes," she said. "The strong, silent type, right?"

"Exactly."

He kissed her. It was a soft melding of lips at first, but gradually, it became harder, hungrier. Soon, both of them were pulling away, sucking in huge gasps of air.

"Maybe I was a little conservative on that ten-minute estimate." He'd already made a full recovery.

"How many condoms did you buy?" she asked.

He fought back the urge to flush. "Six." And they were all in his wallet. Maybe cocky and hopeful weren't such a bad mix after all.

He'd been in too big a hurry the first time, too preoccupied with holding off to truly enjoy the moment. He was going to make up for that now. Sunday trembled slightly when Patrick gently pushed her legs apart, eased his way down the bed and settled between her knees. With one finger, he touched her clit, enjoying her soft sigh.

"I love when you touch me."

He continued to play with her until she was wet and writhing on the bed in need.

"Please, Pat!"

"Not yet. I want to do something." He leaned forward and sucked her clit into his mouth.

Sunday jerked roughly, but Patrick was prepared. With his hands on her hips, he held her in place as he administered a very different kind of kiss. He savored the tangy taste of her juices, inhaled her sweet scent.

"Are you sore?" he asked before delving deeper into his explorations.

She shook her head. He narrowed his eyes until she relented. "Maybe a little bit. Not enough that I want to stop."

"Even so," he ran his tongue along her slit, "we'll go slowly." He pressed his tongue inside her, loving her cries, her pleas for more. Using his finger on her clit, he tried to discover her hot spots, her pleasure points. He wanted to know how to drive her out of her mind with need.

Sunday screamed when she came and Patrick briefly worried that the neighbors might come to investigate. He dismissed the concern. He was going to marry Sunday McKenna, make her his wife. Hell, he'd drag her before a minister tomorrow if she'd agree.

"Pat?"

"Yeah?"

"Get the condom."

Shit. He wondered if the minister was still awake now. Patrick didn't need to be told twice. He quickly donned a condom.

This time when he pushed into her body, he felt in control, ready to take on the world. They rocked together in time, neither of them in a rush to see the end. Sunday stroked his back, his ass cheeks, as Patrick kissed her, nuzzled his nose against her neck.

Patrick moved slowly, careful to make sure that this time, he didn't come alone. When he felt Sunday reaching the precipice, he rubbed her clit. She jolted beneath him.

"Harder," she pleaded.

Patrick paused a mere second before responding, taking her the way he'd only ever dreamed of possessing a woman. His motions sped up as he drove deeper. Sunday quivered and gasped—then she came.

He couldn't resist the tight clench of her body. He didn't fight it. Instead, he gave himself up to the bliss, the rapture.

It was several moments later before he realized he was lying on his back and Sunday wasn't in the bed.

"Sunday?" he called.

"I'll be back in two seconds. I just need to get something."

He went to the bathroom to clean up then returned to the bed. He closed his eyes for a moment, listening to Sunday move around the house. He wondered what she was doing.

"Pat?" she whispered.

He opened his eyes and wondered if he'd drifted off.

"Are you awake?"

He nodded and pushed himself up, sitting with his back against the headboard. "What's that?"

Sunday produced two shot glasses. "Jameson," she announced as she handed him one, keeping the other for herself. "I felt the need to make a special toast."

Patrick grinned. "Sounds like a fine idea."

Sunday lifted her glass. "To you and me and forever."

She tapped her glass to his, but Patrick grasped her wrist before she could drink. "I have a wee toast of my own, lass. To Conall Brannagh."

Sunday laughed, but she raised her glass. Together, they drank.

PATRICK WATCHED the lights on the tree flicker. Every Christmas Eve of their marriage, he and Sunday had sat together in this room, watching the tree, listening to the excited whispers of their children—who pretended to be asleep—and sharing a drink of whiskey. Their toasts had never changed.

Patrick picked up the almost empty bottle of Jameson and poured out the last small shot. He lifted it.

"To you, Sunday. Merry Christmas, love."

ABOUT THE AUTHOR

Virginia native Mari Carr is a New York Times and USA TODAY bestseller of contemporary erotic romance novels. With over one million copies of her books sold, Mari was the winner of the Romance Writers of America's Passionate Plume award for her novella, Erotic Research. She has over a hundred published works, including her popular Wild Irish and Compass books, along with the Trinity Masters series she writes with Lila Dubois.

Follow Mari:
www.maricarr.com
mari@maricarr.com

Sparks in Texas

Sparks Fly

Waiting for You

Something Sparked

Off Limits

No Other Way

Whiskey Eyes

Trinity Masters

Elemental Pleasure

Primal Passion

Scorching Desire

Forbidden Legacy

Hidden Devotion

Elegant Seduction

Secret Scandal

Delicate Ties

Beloved Sacrifice

Masterful Truth

Masters Admiralty

Treachery's Devotion

Loyalty's Betrayal

Pleasure's Fury

Honor's Revenge

Bravery's Sin

Wild Irish

Come Monday

Ruby Tuesday

Waiting for Wednesday

Sweet Thursday

Friday I'm in Love

Saturday Night Special

Any Given Sunday

Wild Irish Christmas

Wild Irish Box Set

Wilder Irish

Wild Passion

Wild Desire

Wild Devotion

Wild at Heart

Wild Temptation

Wild Kisses

Wild Fire

Wild Spirit

Cowboys!

Spitfire

Rekindled

Inflamed

Big Easy

Blank Canvas

Crash Point

Full Position

Rough Draft

Triple Beat

Winner Takes All

Going Too Fast

Boys of Fall

Free Agent

Red Zone

Wild Card

Clandestine

Bound by the Past

Covert Affairs

Scoring

Mad about Meg

Cocktales

Party Naked

Screwdriver

Bachelor's Bait

Screaming O

Crossed Wires

Taming His Princess

Claiming Her Cowboy

Finding Her Master

Sharing Their Lover

June Girls

No Recourse

No Regrets

Just Because

Because of You

Because You Love Me

Because It's True

Love Lessons

Happy Hour

Slam Dunk

Madison Girls

Kiss Me Kate

Three Reasons Why

Scoundrels

Black Jack

White Knight

Red Queen

What Women Want

Sugar and Spice

Everything Nice

Individual Titles

Seducing the Boss

Erotic Research

Tequila Truth

Power Play

Rough Cut

Assume the Position

Do Over